A Bookshop in Algiers

A Bookshop in Algiers

Kaouther Adimi

*translated from the French
by Chris Andrews*

First published in Great Britain in 2020 by
Serpent's Tail,
an imprint of Profile Books Ltd
29 Cloth Fair
London
ECIA 7JQ
www.serpentstail.com

First published in the United States of America in 2020 by New Directions as *Our Riches*

Originally published in French as *Nos richesses*

Please see acknowledgements and permissions on p.146

10 9 8 7 6 5 4 3 2 1

Printed and bound in Great Britain by Clays Ltd, Elcograf S.p.A.

A CIP catalogue record for this book is available from the British Library.

ISBN 978 1 78816 469 6
eISBN 978 1 78283 665 0

FSC
www.fsc.org
MIX
Paper from
responsible sources
FSC® C018072

TO THE PEOPLE OF RUE HAMANI

El Biar
I go down to the port
by the Télemly path
blazing in the sun.
Rue Charras smells of anisette.
I leaf through a book
at Les Vraies Richesses.

   —Frédéric Jacques Temple, "Distant Landscapes"

A day will come when the very stones cry out at the utmost
injustice done to the people of this land . . .

   —Jean Sénac, "Letter from a Young Algerian Poet
to All His Brothers"

Algiers, 2017

As soon as you arrive in Algiers, you will have to tackle the steep streets, climb and then descend. You will come out onto Didouche Mourad—so many alleyways off to each side, like hundreds of intersecting stories—a few steps away from a bridge that is favored by suicides and lovers alike.

Keep going down, away from the cafés and the bistros, the clothing stores, the produce markets, quick, keep going, don't stop, turn left, smile at the old florist, lean for a few moments against a hundred-year-old palm tree, ignore the policeman who will tell you it's prohibited, run after a goldfinch along with some kids, and come out onto Place Emir-Abdelkader. You might miss the Milk Bar: in full daylight the letters on the recently renovated façade are hard to make out. Their contours are blurred by the blinding sun and the almost-white blue of the sky. You will see children climbing onto the plinth of the statue of Emir Abdelkader, smiling broadly, posing for their parents, who will waste no time in posting the photos on social media. A man will be smoking and reading a newspaper in a doorway. You will have to greet him and exchange a few pleasantries before turning back, but not before glancing off to the side: the silver sea sparkling, the cries of the gulls, and always that blue, almost white.

You will have to follow the channel of sky, forget the Haussmann-style buildings, and go past the Aéro-habitat, that block of cement looming over the city.

You will be alone; you have to be alone to get lost and see everything. There are some cities, and this is one, where any kind of company is a burden. You wander here as if among thoughts, hands in your pockets, a twinge in your heart.

You will climb the streets, push open heavy wooden doors that are never locked, touch the marks left on the walls by bullets that cut down unionists, artists, soldiers, teachers, anonymous passers-by, and children. For centuries the sun has been rising over the terraces of Algiers, and for centuries, on those terraces, we have been killing each other.

Take the time in the Casbah to sit down on a step. Listen to the young banjo players, imagine the old women behind closed shutters, watch the children having fun with a cat that's lost its tail. And the blue overhead, and the blue at your feet: sky blue plunging into sea blue, a drop of oil dilating to infinity. The sea and sky that we no longer notice, in spite of the poets, trying to convince us that they are palettes of color, waiting to be adorned with pink or yellow or black.

Forget that the roads are drenched with red, a red that has not been washed away, and every day our steps sink into it a little deeper. At dawn, before cars have invaded all the city's thoroughfares, we can hear bombs exploding in the distance.

But you will follow the alleys that lie open to the sun, won't you? You'll come at last to Rue Hamani, formerly known as Rue Charras. You'll look for 2b: it won't be easy, because some of the numbers have disappeared. You'll stand there facing a sign in a window: *One who reads is worth two who don't*. Facing History, with a capital *H*, which changed this world utterly, but also the small-*h* history of a man, Edmond Charlot, who, in 1936, at the age of twenty-one, opened a lending library called Les Vraies Richesses.

1

The morning of the last day. The night has withdrawn, uneasily. The air is thicker, the sunlight grayer, the city uglier. The sky is crowded with heavy clouds. The stray cats are on the lookout, ears pricked. The morning of a last day, like a day of shame. The fainter-hearted among us hurry past, pretending not to know what's going on. Children lingering curiously are tugged away by their parents.

At first, there was a deep silence in Rue Hamani, formerly Rue Charras. It's rare, that sort of calm in a city like Algiers, always restless and noisy, perpetually buzzing, complaining, moaning. In the end, the silence was broken by men pulling the metal grille down over the window of Les Vraies Richesses, the bookstore. Well, it hasn't been a bookstore since the 1990s when the Algerian government bought it from Madame Charlot, the original owner's sister-in-law: it's just been an annex of the National Library of Algiers, a nameless place that passers-by rarely even stop to look at. Still, we go on calling it Les Vraies Richesses, the way we went on saying Rue Charras for years, instead of Rue Hamani. We are the people of this city and our memory is the sum of all our stories.

An eager young journalist on assignment writes in a notebook with a black cover: *It held out for eighty years!* Eyes like a weasel, we think suspiciously. Little careerist, we can smell you a mile off: the store deserves better. *Not many people, sad sky, sad city, sad iron curtain in front of the books,* he adds, before changing his mind and crossing out *sad city.* The effort of thinking creases his face almost painfully. He is just starting out in the profession. His father, who owns a big plastics firm, made a deal with the editor in chief: he'd take out ads if they took on his son. From our windows, we observe this awkward rookie. *Wedged between a pizzeria and a grocery, the old bookstore Les Vraies Richesses, once the haunt of famous writers.* He chews on his pen and scribbles in the margin. *(There was Camus, but who are the others in the photos pinned up inside the store? Edmond Charlot, Jean Sénac, Jules Roy, Jean Amrouche, Himoud Brahimi, Max-Pol Fouchet, Sauveur Galliéro, Emmanuel Roblès ... No idea. Look them up.) A plant has been left outside, on the little step where the young Albert Camus used to sit and edit manuscripts. No one is going to take it away. Last survivor (or last witness?). This bookstore / library was kept in perfect order: its handsome storefront window shines like a sky full of stars (is that a cliché? Check.)* He adds a period and starts a new paragraph. *The Ministry of Culture declined to answer our questions. Why sell off a branch library to a private buyer? Does no one care that we are losing a chance to read, a chance to learn? One who reads is worth two who don't. That is what is written in French and Arabic on the window, but those who don't read are worth nothing.* He crosses out the last sentence and continues: *In these times of economic crisis, the government has seen fit to sell such places to the highest bidder. For years it has wasted oil revenue and now the ministers cry: "It's a crisis," "there is no alternative," "it's not a priority; people need bread, not books; sell the libraries, sell the bookstores." The government is sacrificing culture to build mosques on every street corner! There was a time when books were so precious that we treated them with respect, we promised them to children, we gave them as gifts to our loved ones!*

Happy with this draft of his article, the journalist walks away, pen in pocket, gripping his black notebook, without even a glance at Abdallah, who used to check out books at Les Vraies Richesses, the bookseller, as we call him. There he is, alone on the sidewalk in Rue Charras. He's over six feet tall, and still an imposing figure although he now has to use a wooden walking stick. He is wearing a blue shirt and gray trousers. On his shoulders he is carrying a white sheet of coarse Egyptian cotton, clean if a little yellowed. His face is wrinkled, his skin pale, the line of his mouth firm and clear. He says nothing. He only stares at the storefront window with his large, black, penetrating eyes. Abdallah is proud, a man of few words; he grew up in Kabylia at a time when people did not speak of their feelings. And yet, if the journalist had taken the time to interview him, the old man might have explained, in his deep and soothing voice, what the store means to him and why his heart is broken today. Of course he wouldn't speak of a broken heart; he would find other words. He would stress other feelings, tinged with anger, while keeping the white sheet, as always, firmly wrapped around his shoulders. But the journalist is already far away, whistling in his office, hammering at his keyboard. He is unaware of how his whistling irritates his colleagues, who exchange knowing looks.

The gray glow of the winter sun struggles to illuminate Rue Hamani, formerly Rue Charras. The storekeepers take their time to open up; there's no rush. An underwear store, a grocery, a restaurant, a butcher's, a hairdresser, a pizzeria, a café ... We greet Abdallah with a nod or a gentle squeeze of the arm. We know what he's feeling. Here, we all know what a last day is like. Children cross the street, ignoring the recently repainted pedestrian crossings and the drivers honking at them from their cars made in France, Germany or Japan: an international parade. The high school students, carrying backpacks tagged by their friends, smoke and flirt. The elementary school boys are dressed in blue shirts buttoned up to the neck, the girls in pink smocks. They shout, laugh, and whisper, call out to each other. A schoolboy bumps Abdallah, mumbles an apology, and tilts his head back to meet the eyes of the great big man, before running off to join his older sister, who threatens him with a slap if he doesn't hurry up. "Filthy little brats," yells a woman with a big head and her hair tied back untidily. Equipped with a broom and a bucket of gray water giving off a chemical smell, she scrubs the sidewalk. One of the children gives her the finger. "You asked for it," she says and whoosh, she throws the bucket of dirty water at him. He tries to dodge, but the water splashes onto the legs of his beige cotton trousers. "I'm telling my mother!" he yells, and runs off toward the school. Then the street is calm again and oddly dim. Anxiously, the storekeepers examine the sky. We are not used to this absence of sunlight. "It's a hard winter coming, and many of the homeless won't make it through," says Moussa, who runs the pizzeria next door to Les Vraies Richesses. He is known throughout the neighborhood for his generosity and the birthmark on his face, in the shape of Africa.

This morning, for the first time in twenty years, thinks Abdallah, leaning on his stick, Moussa won't be coming over with his cup of black coffee. Abdallah never allowed him to bring it into Les Vraies Richesses, for fear he might stain the books. At the end of the day, he knows, a little girl will come with her mother to choose books for the week. Pink skirt, white cardigan, shiny shoes, hair in a bunch on one side. She will find the door closed.

We used to see Abdallah through the immaculate storefront window, busily waging his war on red ants. Sometimes, local teenagers would wait until his back was turned and pinch some books, messing up his shelves. He'd let it go, shrug his shoulders and say to Moussa: "Well, if it gets them reading . . ." His friend knew that the books would be resold at a nearby market, but couldn't bring himself to tell Abdallah.

In the neighborhood, we like this solitary old man. What can we tell you about him? We don't know his age. Nor does he. It can only be estimated. When Abdallah came into the world, his father was in

France, working in a factory in the north. Nobody went to register the birth. Which is why, on the bookseller's papers, next to "date of birth," it says: "Unknown, between ..." His age can be guessed from his walking stick, and his hands, which have grown shakier, from the way he strains to hear and speaks more loudly now.

Abdallah's wife died in the dark decade, just before he came to Rue Hamani. When? Where? None of us could say. It isn't customary here to ask a man about his wife, whether she's alive or dead, beautiful or ugly, loved or hated, veiled or not. As far as we know, he has only one child, a married daughter living in Kabylia.

When Abdallah started working at Les Vraies Richesses, we measured the bookstore for him: seven yards wide by four deep. He would stretch out his arms and joke that he could almost touch both walls. On the second floor, up a steep set of stairs, he made himself a rough-and-ready bed with a mattress and two good thick blankets. There has never been any heating. He also acquired an electric hot plate, a tiny refrigerator, and an extra lamp. He performed his ablutions and washed his clothes in the bookstore's little bathroom.

Before, he had worked in an office at the city hall, where he was in charge of stamping papers. He applied his stamp to all manner of documents day in, day out. Luckily, his colleagues liked him and took the time to chat. In 1997, after the death of his wife, he was transferred, at his own request, to the bookstore and given a document stating that he would remain there until he reached retiring age. Which he eventually did. But he had been forgotten. No one came to replace him. Unable to abandon the premises and having no plans or place to go, he stayed on without ever complaining or saying a word to anyone.

That is all we know about this man.

One day the first official letters came, informing him that 2b Rue Hamani had been sold to a developer and that Les Vraies Richesses would soon be closed. Naively, he thought he could persuade the representatives of the state that it was important to keep the place open. He called the Ministry of Culture but he could never get through. The line was always busy and there was no way to leave a message because the answering machine was full. When he went there, the security guard laughed in his face. At the National Library, they heard him out patiently, then led him to the door without a word, without a promise. When the new owner came to visit Les Vraies Richesses, Abdallah asked him what he was planning to do with the bookstore. "Gut it, get rid of those old shelves, and repaint the walls so my nephew can set up a beignet shop. Every kind of beignet you can think of: with sugar, apple, chocolate. We're near the university; the potential's huge. I hope you'll be one of our first customers."

Startled by the cries, we came running to find the owner getting to his feet and dusting off his suit. Abdallah was brandishing his fist and shouting. He wasn't going to let anyone destroy Charlot's bookstore. The owner sneered: "Don't be a clown." He didn't come back but the letters kept arriving, reminding Abdallah that he would soon have to go. He showed them to the young lawyers who came to Moussa's place at lunchtime for pizza squares. They shook their heads and tapped him on the shoulder. "You can't fight the State, *El Hadj*, you know that, and anyway, it's not a bookstore, it's just a branch of the National Library. You admit yourself that no one uses it. How many borrowers do you have? Two or three, right? Is it really worth fighting for? You're old, give it up. The place is tiny, let them have it, there's nothing you can do," they said.

"So they can sell off whatever they like? A bookstore today, a hospital tomorrow? And I just have to shut up?"

Ill at ease, with nothing left to say, the young lawyers ordered more pizza and lemonade.

The day before the closure, Abdallah had an attack. His heart was hammering; it really felt as if it were about to jump out of his chest. He managed to open the door of the bookstore before collapsing on the threshold. His vision dimmed. He could hear the sound of running steps. Running away. Then others approaching. He thought of the pan of water that would soon begin to boil upstairs. He looked up at the big photo on the ceiling of the man who had created that place: Edmond Charlot. Abdallah thought he was dying. And to judge from the trembling glimmer in the eyes of the children gathering around him, so did they.

Moussa didn't have a telephone; he had always been wary of technology. When he heard the cries, he put the hot coffee pot down on the table without a thought for the mark it would leave on the waxed cloth. He took his stick and went out to find a small crowd gathered. The ambulance wouldn't arrive in time. Some young guys from the neighborhood carried Abdallah to the grocer's van and drove him to the hospital. They did what they could to help him hold on, the old guardian of the books, calling on God, who is our first and last resort here. Abdallah was struggling to breathe. Convulsions seized his body and his eyes bulged. The rattling van drove at top speed through the streets of Algiers, swerving to avoid potholes, speed humps, and stray dogs. Treating the old man as if he were an animal soon to be put down, the doctor at the hospital told him to leave Algiers. "This city has its own rules, you can't go against them, it'll kill you in the end. Leave, there's nothing more for you to do here."

Abdallah went back to the bookstore. Wrapped in his white sheet, he lay down on the mezzanine at Les Vraies Richesses. Just before falling asleep, he remembered his first night there, and how he couldn't believe that he was in a place like that, a man like him, who hadn't been able to go to school before the country's independence, who had learned to read Arabic at the mosque, and French, oh but that was much later on, and with great difficulty.

Since the closure, Abdallah has slept in a tiny room attached to the pizzeria next door. It's where they keep the flour, the yeast, the crates of tomatoes, the drums of oil, and the jars of olives. Now there's a sponge-rubber mattress too, and a few cushions. Moussa hasn't told the owner that he is giving shelter to a friend. The book-seller spends all his waking hours standing on the pavement with the white sheet around his shoulders, propped on his walking stick. His eyes are moist, and the ruin of this man's final years is a shame on all the city.

We take turns to make sure that he has what he needs. The lawyers have started going to another neighborhood for lunch, so they won't have to face Abdallah and his endless questions.

And one night, while the young are down in the street, in front of their apartment buildings, solving the world's problems, twenty-year-old Ryad arrives, with the key to Les Vraies Richesses in his pocket.

Algeria, 1930

O ne of the men has a twelve-year-old son who has learned to read French at the School for Native Boys. They stand in a circle around him, smoking quietly. He shows them the front page of the *Petit Journal illustré* dated May 4, 1930, sold for fifty centimes. It's a poster for the centenary of Algeria. The headline, in large, bold, capital letters, reads ALGERIA: FRENCH FOR A HUNDRED YEARS. The boy doesn't dare go on, scared by the suddenly serious looks on the faces of the men, who have even stopped smoking. His father encourages him with a gesture. Slowly, he deciphers the subtitle: "From the conquest of Algiers to the present day, within a century the Barbary Coast has been transformed into a rich and prosperous province." The newspaper is passed around the circle. The men snort as they examine the illustration: a French regiment landing on a deserted coast in 1830. They've erased everything: the Casbah, the port, the gardens, the houses, cafés, markets, inns, but also businesses, bridges, fountains, barracks, trees, language, religion ... "The Centenary Cantata" sung before Gaston Doumergue, President of the Republic, in May 1930 at the Algiers Opera House tells the same story: before the arrival of the French, all was barbarity.

The men speak quietly:

"How long are we going to hang our heads? The Native Code makes us second-class citizens in our own country. This is our home, our land."

"We have to fight, and demand our rights; we have to get organized."

The boy is careful not to draw attention to himself; he knows that the slightest movement will remind the men of his presence, and make them clam up.

"They'll throw us in jail or send us to New Caledonia."

We are the natives, the Muslims, the Arabs. Only a handful of us can educate our children when by some miracle there is a place available in one of the rare native schools. And then we have to be able to do without the child's help on the farm, the farm that belongs to one of the big colonial clans. The clans that make up a powerful lobby, controlling the whole country. No one in Paris cares much about us, us or the thousands of families who have come since the start of colonization, from France, Spain, and Italy, to live in the working-class neighborhoods.

The Centenary is a chance to reinforce colonial authority. It is celebrated in pomp on both sides of the sea. Exhibitions are organized. The politicians who come to Algeria are greeted with proud and beaming smiles. Dances are held on village squares. The women wear cotton dresses; the men wear jackets with broad lapels. Laughter resounds late into the night. Writers sing the sunlight and the joy of living in Algeria. As for us, we shrug our shoulders because we can't read what they write, and anyway we know it's all lies. They say that we believe in all kinds of superstitions, that we are picturesque, that we live in tribes and cannot be trusted. They are annoyed by the swarms of children who mill around the passengers coming ashore, offering to carry their suitcases in the hope of earning a little spare change. The first classes of native schoolmasters are photographed at the teaching college. Not until 1921 are they allowed to wear the same uniform as their European counterparts: the navy blue tunic lightened by a few stripes of sky blue and a white collar. And the finishing touch: a black tie. For us, they chose a fez with a violet tassel, an orange jacket, and a green belt. We are shown off because we look like figures from an oriental postcard; we become exotic in our own country. Jean Guillemin, director of the teachers' college, writes a report on the reorganization of native education. On March 20, 1923, he alerts the inspector of the Algiers education board to the potential danger of mixing native and French students. He is eminent. His expression is grave. His mission is of the utmost importance: to ensure that the two communities coexist in the school system without coming into contact. He recommends separate streams, since it would be too humiliating if a native student were to outperform a French student in the same class. Jean Guillemin is concerned about the self-esteem of certain students.

All is well. It's the Centenary. Charlie Chaplin opens the Aletti, an art deco hotel built at great expense. All is well. The sun shines brightly; the Mediterranean is beautiful; large colonial houses are going up, with their gardens laid out around them. And in Algiers, the President of the Republic listens to his opera, content with the Centenary that glorifies the power of the nation in his charge. He is pleased that the natives have been involved in the organization of the event. He is unaware, or unwilling to know, that they felt underrepresented. All is well. We are not yet making enough noise to disturb the festivities. The police have locked up or deported native activists and politicians. All is well. And yet the sky is strangely dark, and large black clouds mass overhead.

The father takes his son by the hand and leads him through a maze of narrow streets. "You have to go home, straightaway; your mother will be worried. Hurry up."

Edmond Charlot's Notebook
Algiers, 1935–1936

June 12, 1935

I will be bald. That's one thing I can be sure of, at the age of twenty-one. I comb my thinning hair over my scalp before philosophy class with Jean Grenier at the Algiers lycée. He's incredible. He doesn't teach, he tells stories. We never know what to expect when he starts talking. He thinks along with us and gets us to push our thinking to the limit. One day we asked him about his latest book, and he took us on an imaginary tour around the islands that are mentioned in it. I've come a long way from that prison-house of a Jesuit school where I studied up to the eleventh grade.

July 23, 1935

Back in Algiers after a short trip to Paris. Talked with my father in the kitchen till late. I told him how deeply I admire Adrienne Monnier. I got a chance to visit her extraordinary lending library, La Maison des amis des livres, at 7 Rue de l'Odéon. Hundreds and hundreds of volumes! They have everything! And what an extraordinary woman Madame Monnier is ... She told me that she started out with just a few thousand francs. It's what we need in Algeria. My father agrees, but on a smaller scale, he said. Yes, a smaller scale, as long as it's in the same spirit. That is: a store selling new and secondhand books, which is also a lending library, and not just a business but a place where people come to talk and read. A sort of meeting place for friends, but with a Mediterranean outlook too: bringing together writers and readers from all the Mediterranean countries, regardless of language or religion, people from all around this sea. And we really have to take a stand against the Algerianists. We have to think bigger!

September 18, 1935

Grandfather Joseph is back from Ghardaïa. At dinner, he was telling me how he had delivered a camel team to a place in the desert, accompanied by a big-game hunter to protect him against bandit attacks. Odd man: trading is his life, and the stories he tells are largely invented. Grandmother was shaking her head in exasperation. We stayed up late drinking and talking about literature and art. He gave me a copy of Roland Dorgelès's *Wooden Crosses*, signed by the author, and told me that before it won the Prix Femina, it had been shortlisted for the Goncourt, but lost out to Proust in the last round. All the same, his publisher put a publicity strip on the book that read: *Prix Goncourt: 4 votes out of 10.* Grandfather never studied, but I'm amazed by all the things he knows. Grandmother went to bed early, but first she made me promise to go to the Sainte-Eugène cemetery with her on Sunday, to visit my mother's grave.

October 9, 1935

When I was putting books on my shelves, I found ten boxes of breath mints left over from a summer when I used to sell them to stores in the city. I went round to all the grocers, in a short-sleeved shirt, under the burning sun, trying to make a bit of pocket money. It would take me a year at least to finish this lot. I'll give some to my friends. Do mints have an expiration date, or are they good forever, like books?

October 14, 1935

I helped the lady next door to bring in her shopping. She thanked me and said I was very kind, but added that I had a birdlike stare, like an eagle, no less, as if I wanted to gobble her up. Just as well you're smiling, she said, otherwise I'd be frightened. Always a pleasure to hear that sort of thing. I pretended not to take offense and pushed my glasses up to the bridge of my nose to give myself a nonchalant air.

November 6, 1935

Grenier asked each of us what we hope to do when we finish our studies. I said that I was fascinated by the printed word. He observed that there is an opening for a bookseller and publisher in Algiers, and said I should seize the opportunity. I told him that I didn't have the means to set myself up in business. "When two or three people get together," he said, "with a bit of determination, they can easily achieve things that might have seemed impossible." And he added: "If you do start publishing, I'll give you something to help you along." I offered him some mints. He thought that was funny.

December 24, 1935

Nostalgic, depressed. I went through the box of family photos that my father keeps in his desk drawer. The humidity has damaged them slightly: there's one of my great-grandfather, a ship's baker, who came to Algiers with the French fleet in 1830. And one of my parents on their wedding day. The date is inscribed on the back in pencil: "April 6, 1912, Algiers," nothing more specific. Victor Charlot looking tough and proud: mustache like an upside-down V, tightly knotted tie. And Marthe Lucia Grima: beautiful, so beautiful, and ill at ease. Twenty-three and eighteen, respectively. And then an old press cutting dated August 5, 1919: my mother's death notice. Just glanced at it, couldn't bear to read it line by line: *Monsieur Victor Charlot and his two sons, Edmond and Pierre ... deepest sorrow that we inform you ... sad loss ... wife, mother, daughter ... died at Kouba ... in her twenty-sixth year ... funeral, which will be held today ... four-thirty p.m. ... Villa Hélène, Kouba, Oasis stop ... church of Saint-Augustin ... Saint-Eugène cemetery.* Had to pull myself together. Literature, at least, will never abandon me. My father brought me some books. I don't know how I'd ever satisfy my appetite for reading if he wasn't in charge of book distribution at Hachette.

January 6, 1936

I was thinking again about what Professor Grenier said. I mentioned it to some friends. Jean Pane and Madame Couston (as she insists on being called since her husband died) are very enthusiastic. I dream about it day and night.

February 12, 1936

At dinner, my grandmother handed me a slip of paper she had found when she was tidying up. There was a mischievous little smile on her face. It was a note from one of my old teachers at the Jesuit school: *Difficult student; head in the clouds.* I take this as support for my decision not to go to university so that I can dedicate myself fully to literature.

March 2, 1936

I keep doing all sorts of calculations. I don't have much saved up: just the bit of money I earned giving lessons at a business school.

March 4, 1936

Madame Couston doesn't want to get too involved: she doesn't have much time because she has to raise her children on her own. I've managed to scrape together 12,000 francs. That will have to do for what we're hoping to set up: a publishing house, a bookstore, and the rest! We might not be facing deserts or panthers, but it's an adventure all the same.

March 9, 1936

Talked to various members of the family, who are supportive even if they're disappointed by my choice. They could already see me working in the postal service. But I think I glimpsed a little spark of pride in my father's eyes; he can't afford to lend me any money, but he's promised to give me all the unsold books he can pick up at Hachette. My brother, Pierre, was enthusiastic. Grandfather doesn't understand. For him, books are a wonderful way to occupy leisure but they have nothing to do with work. "Look what your father earns, a pittance ..." He thinks I'm going off the rails; I even heard him saying to my grandmother that if I was really determined to sell something, I should go into wine or fruit.

March 11, 1936

Spent the afternoon on the premises of the African Musical Society, over in Belcourt, with student actors from the recently established Workers' Theater: Sicard, Camus, Poignant, Bourgeois. They're frantically rehearsing *Revolt in Asturias*, a play in four acts, which they've sketched out together. The action takes place during the workers' uprising in Spain, in a little town divided into two: on one side, the bourgeoisie; on the other, the proletarians. They're all together in a café listening to the radio, waiting for the election results. The right-wing party wins. At the same time, we learn that striking miners are occupying the town; they're armed. Some storekeepers are killed, a truck explodes ... The government sends in the army and bombers to cut the miners down. The play is brilliant, sharp, scathing. It's going to be a hit, for sure. The money they make will be donated to charities for children in need, European and Arab.

April 17, 1936

Amazing stroke of luck: there's a store to let at 2b Rue Charras, right next to the university. It's tiny: about seven yards by four, but we'll be fine there. Jean Pane, Madame Couston, and I had fun trying to touch both walls with our outstretched arms. A very steep, creaky staircase—I'll wax it—leads up to what we have pretentiously dubbed "the second floor." In fact, it's a little, closet-like space that we're planning to turn into an office by setting up a plank on trestles. I'm happy! I've got no money left, I'm deep in debt, but I'm happy.

April 20, 1936
Meeting with Emmanuel Andreo who has taken over Victor Heintz's old printing works at 41 Rue Mogador. Very interesting conversation: he's a good man, keen to be involved in my projects, and he has faith in the young. He encouraged me to seek out new work, to read, to create. We agreed to do great things together.

April 21, 1936
Camus wants me to print *Revolt in Asturias* immediately. The authors are furious and desperate: the mayor of Algiers, Augustin Rozis, has decided to shut down the play. A sensitive subject; it could stir up unrest. The mayor is afraid of four literature students! More than two months of work down the drain. And now the troupe has to pay all the expenses: six hundred francs just for the set. I agreed, of course. If the play can't be performed, it should at least be read. Camus is also planning to distribute a little red tract, which, he said, will start like this:

WORKERS' THEATER GAGGED
Municipality Takes Fright at
"REVOLT IN ASTURIAS"
Authorized by the Prefect, Banned by the Mayor.
Without a Reason: Arbitrarily.

April 28, 1936
Revolt in Asturias will be published in a few weeks. The dedication reads: "To Algiers, for the friends of the Workers' Theater.

To Sánchez, Santiago, Antonio, Ruiz, and León." The authors are not named. I'm choosing the paper, the fonts, the colors. The red characters of the title will have a really striking effect. Too risky to publish it under my own name; they could come to the store and seize it. After thinking it over, I decided to use my initials, in lower case and italics: *e. c.*

May 5, 1936

This will be a library, a bookstore, a publishing house, but above all a place for friends who love the literature of the Mediterranean. As soon as I took possession, I was overjoyed. I'm starting to meet the neighbors, the storekeepers, the waiters. These are the characters in my new world. *Revolt in Asturias* is on sale. People are saying that *e. c.* stands for Éditions Camus. They'll see through the ruse soon enough, but we're in no hurry to set the record straight; the main thing is, the play is selling.

May 9, 1936

A letter came yesterday from Jean Giono! The great Giono. Without getting my hopes up, I had written to ask for his permission to call the bookstore Les Vraies Richesses, after one of his books, which dazzled me, a book in which he urges us to return to the true riches, that is, the land, the sun, the streams, and finally literature too (land and literature: what could be more important?)— I almost tore the letter as I was opening it, I was so excited. I told Jean Pane what he'd written in reply: "Of course you can use the title. It doesn't belong to me."

June 30, 1936

Heat and humidity. The cicadas are singing under my window. Strange dreams last night: lions and panthers devouring my books. A woman—beautiful, of course—reading on the second floor of my store. Friends seated in curious floating armchairs, laughing in the warm evening light of Rue Charras.

July 19, 1936

I found a wonderful story by Giono in a tourist magazine. "The Roundness of Days": an evocative title. I was carried away, immersed in Provence and the south of France. It's perfect for the store. It matches my vision: a Mediterranean perspective that goes beyond the harbor of Algiers. I wrote to Giono again to ask if he would allow me to reprint the text and offer it to my first customers as a souvenir of the opening.

August 8, 1936

Spent the afternoon getting ready for the opening of Les Vraies Richesses with Jean Pane and Madame Couston. We thought long and hard about a slogan that would sum up our ambitions, and in the end we agreed on: "The young, by the young, for the young." It's pretentious, we know, but after all we *are* young, and it has a defiant ring to it, like a challenge to the staid city of Algiers. We'll have the motto printed in black letters on a big white sign; I've ordered it already.

August 27, 1936

A reply from Giono. What a generous man! He says yes, of course, he's touched. It's at the printer's now: 350 copies on bond paper, for my first 350 clients. Am I being too ambitious? No, this is going to work!

September 9, 1936

Lucienne, the widow of the journalist Victor Barrucand, dropped in to visit the future bookstore. She told me that she has some drawings by Bonnard, for a book that Victor was working on. She has agreed to lend them to me, so I can exhibit them on the day of the opening. Bookstore, publishing house, and now art gallery! She also introduced me to Bonnard's nephew, who's a winemaker, in Rue Charras, just nearby. And he, in turn, agreed to lend me three paintings. I'm so proud!

September 13, 1936

I'm spending a lot of time imagining designs for the books I'm going to publish: the covers, the fonts. For *The Roundness of Days*, I'm having fun arranging the letters of the title in a perfect circle. It will look splendid, I think.

October 1, 1936

Aching back, sweaty face, broken fingernails. For two days, I've been shifting all the books I possess from home to 2b. I'm making labels to stick on the spines and drawing up alphabetical lists of the authors. The place is still almost empty, but you have to hope, at least for a start.

October 5, 1936

Only a month to go before the big day. We've sent out the invitations. My father brought dozens of extra books that he was able to get from work, which fill out my collection nicely.

November 3, 1936

Opening day! Up at dawn. Mild, early-winter weather. A thin Arab waiter, with a drawn face, kind eyes, and a handsome black mustache warned me not to be fooled: a harsh winter's coming, and many of the homeless won't make it through. It sounded as if he were prophesying the end of the world. I went to the store with my heart in my mouth. What if no one comes?

November 19, 1936

Since the opening, customers keep crowding in to Les Vraies Richesses to borrow or buy. They're never in a hurry; they want to talk about everything: the writers, the color of the covers, the size of the fonts ... Teachers, students, and artists mainly, but a few workers who've put some money aside to buy a novel, too. The big adventure has begun.

December 24, 1936

An article in the *L'Écho d'Alger* about Les Vraies Richesses, just before Christmas.

December 25, 1936

Read *Sea Salt* by Gabriel Audisio, from Marseille, whose father was the director of the Algiers Opera. Brimful of youth and Tunisian sunlight. Long live the Mediterranean! I must write to Audisio. Maybe he'll let me have something to publish.

December 31, 1936

A lot to think about: anticipating orders, noting down the addresses of the printers people tell me about, appointments I mustn't forget. And of course, making sure to record the titles of the books sent to the printer, the costs we agreed on, the print runs, the delivery dates. I also have to take packages to the post office, pay the bills, keep an eye on the accounts. It's all part of the publisher's trade, as much as reading manuscripts, maybe even more! I have drawn up two columns in a big ledger for the accounts: expenses on one side, plenty of those (overheads, royalties, printing costs, dues); revenues on the other, much less substantial, only a couple of hundred francs.

2

By the time Ryad arrives in Algiers, on the last flight, night has fallen. His hair is a mess. No one has come to meet him; he doesn't know anyone here. Even at this late hour, the airport is full of cheerful idlers, plus a few homeless people. We go there to welcome friends and family, but also because we like to watch the travelers preparing for departure. We imagine that one day we too will fly away. Looking distraught and lost, Ryad steps out of the airport. A young man with an acne-ravaged face calls out: "For a thousand dinars, I'll drop you wherever you like."

The unlicensed cab driver turns on the radio to a long monologue about soccer and politics. This leaves Ryad free to look out the window. The road is empty, the city dimly lit, the restaurants all closed. The driver stretches out his arm and points to something in the distance. "Look, over there, you never see any light. It's the Casbah, a black hole." Ryad smiles but doesn't reply. A few minutes later, the taxi slows down, before dropping him off at the start of Rue Hamani, formerly Rue Charras. The neighborhood is quiet and cold; the lights are out. Since it's clear that this one-off fare has no desire to talk, the driver pulls away without another word. Anyway, words, in the middle of the night, we know too well what they can do: the waves of trouble they stir up, breaking and crashing into each other.

Ryad approaches 2b. There is no sign to show what it is. The storefront is dirty. Through the grille he can see a big window, with the motto: *One who reads is worth two who don't*. To the right, a pizzeria, to the left, a grocery, both shut. Sudden barking makes him jump. He has just arrived but he already can tell that he's not going to like this street. He feels in his pocket for the key that he has brought from Paris and inserts it into the lock. The grille going up makes a sinister noise. With a second key, he opens the door. It sticks for a moment, but then it gives. Because of the darkness, he has to proceed gingerly; there's a musty smell, and he's listening for the slightest noise. He's afraid, although he knows that he's alone in the store. He finds the switch and flicks it. The light dazzles him. The walls are covered with hundreds of books. In places, the old shelves are collapsing under their weight. Orange labels identify the various sections: History, Literature, Poetry ... A couple of magazines lie on the dark wooden floor, which is covered with dust. At the back, facing the entrance, stands a solid wooden desk. There are black-and-white photos hung up around the room. Ryad deciphers the names underneath, most of them unknown to him: Albert Camus, Jules Roy, André Gide, Kateb Yacine, Mouloud Feraoun, Emmanuel Roblès, Jean Amrouche, Himoud Brahimi, Mohammed Dib. And in the middle, on the ceiling, surveying the premises, a huge portrait of a bald man smiling slightly, wearing dark glasses, with a look at once crazy and wise. Edmond Charlot.

Wearily, Ryad climbs the little wooden staircase up to the attic room where he knows he will find a mattress. He collapses onto it beneath the ceiling of colored squares: green, red, yellow, blue. Sleep. Tomorrow he'll have to start clearing the place out.

Ryad wakes feeling groggy. He sits up. The suitcase is at his feet. Memories of the metro back in Paris, its squealing brakes, the bus to the airport, the corridors, the people with their heavy bags full of souvenirs, the dirt under his nails, in his pores, at the back of his throat. Dark air, dark clouds. Just as the plane was about to touch down, it began to shudder. A woman shrieked and frightened her baby, who began to cry. Through the window, just before the wheels made contact with the dimly lit tarmac, Ryad thought he saw birds taking flight. Then customs, the ride with the young man whose beard wasn't thick enough to hide his acne. The road at night, the black hole of the Casbah, the little street back from the big one, the bookstore, the old mattress, the blankets with their holes. His cell phone doesn't work here, except to show the time. Seven o'clock. The street will soon wake up. The sky is growing lighter, changing from black to steely gray, as if an eraser were rubbing at it. Cats can be heard fighting. There will never be a morning without a cat fight in Algiers. Ryad imagines the animals hurling themselves at each other beneath the clouds heavy with rain.

Ten days ago, Ryad was coming home from the university on the metro. He leaned his head against the window, trying to withdraw from the racket around him, the singing beggar and the baby crying in its stroller. He was lost in thought and worried: he was getting nowhere in his search for an internship. Dozens of companies had turned him down, with or without a reason. When he reached his station, he got out and went to his usual bar. A charmless place where he knew that he could sit peacefully with his pint of beer and brood. He took his place at the bar beside a man who was already far gone, staring off into nowhere. Ryad felt his cell phone vibrate in the pocket of his jacket. It was an email from his father:

My son,

Your mother was saying you still don't have an internship. You could have one in Algiers. A friend of mine told me that one of his friends has bought an old bookstore downtown. Actually, it's more like a branch library. The people in the neighborhood are very attached to it, even if they don't use it. You know how it is: we don't know what riches we have until they're gone. Anyway, the new owner is planning to turn the place into a restaurant. He's going to sell beignets. All sorts of beignets. I bet he'll do well. A beignet's always going to be easier to sell here than a book. He keeps asking the National Library to come and take the books away, but no one ever gets back to him. He doesn't want to wait any longer, and he needs someone to clear the place out as soon as possible and repaint it. It'll take you a week or two. There's a little mezzanine with a mattress for you to sleep on. My friend will sign the papers for the internship. He'll email you too and send you the keys.

    See you soon,
    Dad

Two days later, Ryad got an email from this friend of his father's:

Hi Ryad,

    How are you doing? Your father tells me you're a man now, all grown up! We can sort out your internship, no problem; we'll sign the agreement and put a stamp on it. I'll be your contact if you run into problems; my friend travels a lot and he doesn't have time to take care of this. Don't leave anything on the premises. Throw it all out or destroy it. Don't talk with the neighbors, especially the storekeepers. The important thing is to get rid of everything in that bookstore and repaint it white, as quickly as possible. I'll send you some money along with the keys, to cover your costs.

    There's a list of all the stuff in the store below.
    Thank you.

List of things to get rid of:
1,009 novels in French by French and foreign authors.
132 novels in French by Algerian authors.
222 novels in Arabic.
17 works on religious themes. *Hide these in a black rubbish bag when you're throwing them out to avoid any problems.*

42 volumes of poetry. *If you have a girlfriend, you can keep one or two of these for her. The rest, in the trash.*

18 scientific works.

9 works of psychology.

26 works of history.

171 children's books.

38 books about theater.

19 books about cinema.

Various black-and-white photographs.

A large color photo portrait.

An oak desk with a jammed drawer and a narrow gap at the top.

An old lamp.

A rusty sign: "The young, by the young, for the young."

A mattress on the mezzanine. *You can sleep on it while you're working there, then throw it out.*

Papers.

A broom.

A bucket.

Ryad has only been to Algiers once before, at the age of six. He went with his father, to visit his uncle. He found the city terrifying. This uncle took Ryad to his daughter's room and told them to play there quietly. Ryad's cousin was a year younger than him but four inches taller. Her head was huge and her chaotic, curly hair seemed to grow straight up. She tied his hands behind his back with a cord and slapped him hard, sneering.

Ever since, Ryad has been wary of this city, and of tall girls with curly hair. He never returned to the capital when he was living in Algeria, and as soon as he had his baccalauréat, he left for Paris to pursue his studies, with the financial support of his father, a pharmacist in Constantine.

And here he is, this morning, in Algiers. The carefully labeled books lining the walls of the store give it a welcoming look, but

Ryad feels uneasy. He has never liked reading, and all this printed, bound and glued paper has no charm at all for him. He sits at the desk, tries to open the drawer, gives up. He goes to the shelves. Some of the books are very big and others are tiny. It's like a multitude of tribes. Some of the covers are torn or stained. Edmond Charlot watches over everything he does. The man in the photo looks amused. This Ryad finds reassuring. He opens the front door. It is still dark; the streetlamps are shining. The buildings are white with gold-painted balconies and blue shutters. A few men walk past in the street, hurriedly, coat collars turned up, heads down, as if counting their steps. It's raining; puddles begin to appear. The rain becomes a mesh. Across from the store, an old man, leaning on a walking stick, a white sheet wrapped around his shoulders. Ryad is puzzled by the sheet.

He steps out, avoiding the old man's gaze, and goes to the grocer's next door. The shelves are half empty and what there is by way of produce lies in random piles. There are bruised apples, lettuces, padlocks by the dozen, long thin red peppers like the ones Ryad's mother used to wave under his nose when he was a child, threatening to make him eat them if he told a lie. There are also transparent plastic sandals, checkered dishcloths sold in threes, and jars of jam with labels that say "100% fruit, 100% sugar." He is greeted by the storekeeper, a smiling man with a handsome gray beard:

"Good morning, *Hbibi*, can I help you?"

"Yes, I need to buy some paint. Would you have any?"

"Oh no, my friend! It won't be easy to find, you know."

"Really?"

"Yes, there's a paint shortage all over the city."

"Since when?"

"Since yesterday."

"And is there more coming?"

"No, not with this crisis. There was a scam, some shady deal between the producers and the distributors. I don't know the details, but if you're after paint in this city, I can tell you now, you won't find any."

"Damn."

"That's how it is. And with the new laws, we're not allowed to import it either."

"So you can't find any paint for me? None at all?"

"Not now, but who knows? Maybe later there'll be a way. You have to wait, and pray, and believe in miracles. Have an apple to cheer you up. On the house."

"Thanks."

Not daring to pick and choose, Ryad reaches for the closest apple. With a worried look on his face, the grocer watches him walk away. We got together this morning before Abdallah woke up. In the middle of the night, the acne-faced driver warned us that he had just dropped off a young man at 2b. We know that the grille has been rolled up. We can guess why Ryad has come; we are aware that Les Vraies Richesses will soon disappear. Within minutes, the news had spread through the neighborhood, and now there's not a single can of paint for sale.

Ryad walks up Rue Hamani. From our windows, we see him stop in front of the café, Chez Saïd, which has just opened. The awning is unfolding. The waiter, a dark, cadaverous guy, hair full of gel, bags under his eyes, his upper lip deformed by chewing tobacco, is getting the plastic chairs down off the tables. Ryad hesitates, but the waiter invites him to take a seat.

"What can I get you?"

"A coffee, please. No sugar."

Ryad tugs on his sleeves to cover his freezing hands. He doesn't remember the city being so cold. He is thinking about the old man in front of the bookstore. Where is he from? Why is he carrying that heavy white sheet on his shoulders? And why was he staring like that, with those dark eyes, like black agate?

A few days ago, Ryad was sitting in another café, in Paris, with Claire. They didn't want to leave, in spite of the cold and the darkness falling. But the waiter kept shifting the tables and looking at them impatiently. In the end, they got up. And the door was shut behind them hurriedly, with relief. Claire and Ryad walked along the banks of the Seine, remembering their recent vacation in Provence: the cicadas waking them up in the morning, the village of red and ochre stone, the fields as far as they could see. Claire was brimming with restlessness, laughter in her eyes. She kept saying she couldn't stand it anymore: the rain, the cold, the fog; her whole body was crying out for the sun. And he watched her, took it all in: the bright eyes, the smile that kept breaking out, then hiding, and breaking out again, her hands that came to rest on his arm, just like that, without a thought.

The waiter at Chez Saïd comes back with a coffee in a big white cup bearing the inscription USMA, an Algiers soccer team.

"It's a bad day. With this weather, we won't have many customers. People are scared of the rain."

Ryad nods. Gray clouds drift overhead. Two men in their sixties, with newspapers under their arms, come and sit down, talking loudly.

"Garlic is one thousand five hundred dinars, can you believe it? Fffff..."

"And did you see the price of bananas? They've gone from sixty dinars to six hundred and eighty in the space of a few months."

"They've used up the oil, and now what? It's a crisis, a real crisis."

"People will be going hungry soon."

"It's serious, what's happening here, my friend, very serious."

"What can we do?"

"Nothing, there's nothing we can do."

"It's sad, what's happening."

"Very sad."

"And you can't say anything, they've gagged everyone."

"That's right, you can't say anything."

"It's the only country in the world where the State holds the people accountable and not the other way around."

"True, too true. They're always blaming us."

"And what are the young people doing? Nothing!"

"Nothing—and they're not going to do anything. My son is twenty and he spends all day in front of his computer, the idiot!"

"Mine sleeps all day. If I so much as open the door, he bellows like a cow getting its throat cut."

"Useless generation!"

"Hey you, kid!"

Ryad turns to the two men.

"Yes?"

"What are you doing, you young ones, hey? What are you waiting for? Why aren't you out in the streets, demonstrating? Why are you so feeble?"

"I don't know."

"*I don't know.*"

The two men burst out laughing and return to their conversation:

"I think they put something in the food."

"Who?"

"The government, they dose the food with illicit substances to soften the brain; that's why we let them push us around. I read a really interesting article about it on a blog."

"Like the date-rape drug?"

"Yes, like that. They must have invented a drug to make us more docile. How else could they do it?"

"But there are people who demonstrate, there are riots all over ... Just yesterday I saw a video on social media. It was in the south, a violent riot. The police beat up a whole lot of young people."

"Sure, but that must be because they're not getting enough to eat down there ... They're drugging us, I tell you."

Ryad gulps his scalding coffee and leaves a few coins on the table. Going back down the street, he stops at a bakery. The woman behind the counter is tiny. Her head is barely visible over the cash register. A violet scarf covers her hair and she is wearing pink eyeshadow.

"Good morning. Could I ..."

"I don't sell paint."

"Excuse me?"

"What do you want?"

"Um ... a croissant. Did you say you don't sell paint?"

"No. There you are, my son. Enjoy it. May God protect you."

The wind shakes the palm fronds. It starts to rain again, gently at first, then with increasing force. Ryad runs to the bookstore. As he ducks in, he notices the old man who was there this morning, with the white sheet still on his shoulders, and rainwater streaming down his face. Children run for cover. Puddles reflect the light of the lamps, and the street begins to glisten. Within a few minutes, it is empty except for Abdallah. Ryad hesitates to beckon to the old man, who seems immense, and slightly mad. In the end, he goes out onto the sidewalk. Under the white sheet, heavy with rain, Abdallah is wearing a brown suit, cheap but clean and still relatively dry.

"*Salam*, my son."

"*Salam, El Hadj*. Don't you want to go home? You'll catch your death standing out in the rain, and that wet sheet must be heavy."

"No, I'm all right here."

Abdallah wraps the drenched sheet more tightly around his body.

"Are you sure? Do you live far away?"

"No, I live here."

He gestures vaguely at the street.

"Here? Outside?"

"No, here, here."

He points at the street again.

"You don't want to come in for a moment? I think I can make you a coffee."

"Come in? To the bookstore?"

"Yes."

"No. I prefer to stay here."

"Is there something I can do for you?"

"No. I can still get around and I've got my stick. What's your name?"

"Ryad."

"I'm Abdallah. Ryad what? Whose son are you?"

"My parents' son."

"Fool. Where are your parents? What do they do? Who knows them?"

"They live in Constantine."

"Ah, you're not from Algiers."

"No one's from Algiers, *El Hadj*, it's a city of foreigners."

"That's true, very true ... Do you like reading?"

"No ... books and me, we ..."

"Books and you, what?"

"We don't really get on."

"Books get on with everyone, little fool."

"Well maybe I don't get on with them. You don't want to come in, *El Hadj*? We have to get out of this rain, it's pouring."

"It's God's blessing."

"We're going to get soaked."

"Look around you. These things have been here for a long time. Centuries. A little bit of water's not going to make them disappear. I've been through a few storms and floods myself. You shouldn't be scared of the rain. What can it do to you?"

"Give you a cold, or flu, or pneumonia."

"You know your diseases but you don't like books; what are you doing in a bookstore?"

"I have to clear it out and repaint it."

"Why?"

"For work."

"Destroying a bookstore, you call that work?"

"It's an internship."

"An internship? You want to be a destroyer of bookstores? What kind of job is that?"

"No, I'm going to be an engineer."

"Engineers build. They don't destroy."

"I have to do a hands-on internship."

"Are you an engineer or a worker?"

"I have to have manual work experience to complete this year of my engineering degree. I empty the place, I repaint it, and I'm gone. No thinking required."

"You've come to a bookstore so you won't have to think?"

"I'm just here to clear it out, not to read the books."

"That's what they teach you? What sort of university is it?"

"It's in Paris."

"Pfff... Now the French are sending us wreckers. 'Worker-engineers,' yes, sir! The locals aren't good enough. Young people these days, all you know how to do is destroy."

"Young people these days ..."

"What?"

"Nothing. 'Young people these days' ... no, forget it. You know, we do what we can with what you've left us."

"Who sent you?"

"No one. I just took the job. Look, I'm cold. We should go in."

"It's not cold. It's in your mind. Who sent you? Who gave you this job? What's his name?"

"I don't know him; he knows someone who knows someone who mentioned it to my father."

"Even to destroy you have to pull strings ... Pfff ... It's the same everywhere: contacts and corruption. From the watchman at the cemetery to the head of state."

"*Aaashooo!*"

"Go inside, my son, you'll get sick. I hope you brought some medicine from France, because all the pills here are made of baking powder: they poison you slowly."

"What about you? Don't you want to come in?"

"No, leave me alone."

* * *

Ryad leaves the old man standing in the rain. He goes into the book-store and sits on the only chair, behind the little wooden desk facing the door. The wind is still blowing, playing its sinister symphony. Through the broad storefront window, Abdallah is visible, leaning on his stick, his silhouette distorted by the white sheet that envelops him like a strange celestial veil.

Algiers, 1939

Sitting on the doorstep of Les Vraies Richesses with a cigarette in his mouth, Albert Camus is editing a manuscript. A few Arab schoolboys go past in the street, wearing mended shirts and gaping shoes. A pastor leads them on. Some of us have entrusted our children to the Christian missions. This, they assure us, is the way out of poverty: they will learn to read and be housed for free. We know that they will not be allowed to speak Arabic or Berber, and will have to attend mass. When they come home for vacations, we inspect them. We check that they remember their language, and the traditions, and our religious principles. They show the few books that they own to their friends who can't go to school, and teach them the letters of the alphabet; they go back to work in the fields or the factories until it is time to return to school.

In Rue Charras, some children who are chasing a ball bump into a woman. "Dirty brats!" she yells. Charlot, joining Camus on the doorstep, watches them with a smile. Little girls are begging on a café terrace. The portly owner grumbles: "There are more and more of them."

Edmond Charlot's Notebook
Algiers, 1937–1939

January 2, 1937

Just as he had promised, Grenier gave me a manuscript with the beautiful title *Santa Cruz and Other African Landscapes*. I read it straight through, I was so impatient! I spent the night doing the layout, with a ruler, a Stanley knife, tracing paper, and the proofs. There's a graduate of the Algiers School of Art whose work I greatly admire: René-Jean Clot. I'm thinking of asking him to draw a frontispiece for the book. The print run will be 550 copies.

January 4, 1937

Dinner with my university friend, Claude de Fréminville. He has just come into a small inheritance, enough to set him up as a printer. Very proud of his business, something I can understand. We'll work together on the books with smaller print runs, the Fréminville Printing Works and Éditions Charlot.

January 17, 1937

I returned the Bonnard drawings. Magnificent work, but I don't think many of the customers appreciated it.

February 9, 1937

We made a poster for the store. It might be too serious. I don't know. I should ask my friends what they think.

> *Fine bindings of works by a select range of authors*
> *An irreproachable choice of books for children*
> *and readers of all ages*
> *Hand-illustrated first editions*
> *Canvases signed by leading painters*
> *Casts by Lorenzi*
> *For a beautiful book:*
> LES VRAIES RICHESSES.

March 12, 1937

Jean Pane wants to leave Algiers and go and live in Kabylia. He has the crazy plan of opening an art school for Kabyle and Arab students. Uncle Albert Grima generously lent me what he could to help me buy Jean's share. Now there are just two of us running the business, Madame Couston and myself. But I shouldn't forget the precious help that many friends have given us. It's their business too, in a way.

March 20, 1937

Evening with my father. A long conversation about paper: the smell, the feel, the difference between new and old. Personally I'm very fond of Japanese paper: it has a subtle ivory color that gives a book character. I much prefer it to vellum paper, which has no texture: it's too smooth, too perfect.

April 1, 1937

My friend Sauveur Galliéro came to see me at the store with Himoud Brahimi, known as Momo, his neighbor in the Casbah. Galliéro looks just like he did in elementary school: always tight around the eyes as if struggling to understand, like a stranger in his own world. Such a talented painter. At school, he was better than the teacher. Today he seemed anxious. The Algiers Academy wants him to exhibit, but of course they're not offering any help or providing a space. He's completely broke and doesn't know which gallery to ask. I offered him the store. We'll put the sculptures on the shelves beside the books, and hang the paintings up high on the walls. The tightness didn't go away, but a smile lit up his face. It will be a success, I know it will. I warmed to Himoud Brahimi immediately (everyone calls him Momo). He's perfectly trilingual: French, Arabic, and Berber. Funny too. He's going to be a great writer, a great poet, a great something anyway.

September 29, 1937
Advertisement in *L'Écho d'Alger*. Two little lines between a cypress tree for sale and a lady living on her own looking for a lodger. *SALE secondhand classics and detective novels.* Les Vraies Richesses, *2b Rue Charras*. People keep telling me they've seen it. I try to connect the advertisements. What if I bought the cypress tree and gave it to the lady who's looking for company? Maybe she has some detective novels. Maybe she's a beauty. With soft, smooth skin. I'm straying.

December 22, 1937
The subscription system is working well: it's popular with students because it allows them to borrow books for a small monthly fee. Sales are not spectacular, but they're holding up. When I arrive at the store in the morning, I pause in front of the little step to contemplate my realm. Sometimes I stand there so long, the waiter at the café next door gets worried and asks me if everything's all right. And yes, everything's all right: the books are arranged in alphabetical order, with the paintings hanging above them, and this space is given over entirely to literature, art, and friendship.

December 28, 1937

Met Emmanuel Roblès, a young man from Oran, Spanish background. He's doing his military service near Algiers. Patient and reserved: a pleasure to talk with him. He told me that he will soon have a book published. I'm very curious to read it.

February 15, 1938

Today I am twenty-three years old. I spent the evening of my birthday behind a desk, sorting out bills, reading letters from customers who would like to order this or that book, addressing envelopes and packages, throwing out useless magazines and advertisements, filling in forms. Boring. It all piles up on my little desk. Each of these tasks has to be done but they're leaving me less and less time for literature, which is the heart of the business after all.

February 27, 1938

Every week, I think about reorganizing the books and the artworks but I can't; there's not enough space in the store.

February 28, 1938

Beautiful article about Grenier's book *Santa Cruz and Other African Landscapes* by Gabriel Audisio in *Cahiers du Sud*. I met the editor, Jean Ballard, in Algiers a year or two ago. He refused to take off his checked overcoat in spite of the stifling heat. A real character. Very commercially minded, unlike me! He persuaded me to approach some companies about taking out ads in his magazine. I failed miserably. Unlike my grandfather, I don't have much of a flair for business.

March 4, 1938

I found Madame Couston crying on the mezzanine. She confessed that she just can't manage, financially, with her children; she has to find a real job. She's bailing out.

March 19, 1938

Ill. The flu has knocked me flat. I have to stay in bed, unfortunately. But I can still read manuscripts. Manon is looking after me. Beautiful Manon: she came and lit up every part of my life, and now I can't imagine it without her.

April 20, 1938

Too much enthusiasm, too many ideas: I'm wearing out the people around me. No end of projects but I really have to rein in my grand ambitions: the meager means at my disposal are bringing me down to earth.

April 23, 1938

Shy students come to the store with their manuscripts: they give me fair copies made out in ink (and carefully keep the precious originals).

May 17, 1938

Lunch with Gabriel Audisio, who's passing through Algiers. Long conversation about publishing and literature. I said that for me what matters is not so much the coherence of the list as publishing work that I admire; when I talk to the press and the public, I need to be able to back every book. My commitment has to be absolute. That's how I see my task. The writer has to sit down and write; the publisher has to give the book a life in the world. This isn't something I can keep in a compartment. Literature is too important for me to spend time on anything else.

May 25, 1938

New address: Rue Lys-du-Parc. Moved out of the family home!

June 7, 1938

Conversation with Camus and Audisio about launching a bimonthly magazine to be called *Rivages*. A space for discussing the work of new writers. We agreed to devote a special issue next year to Federico García Lorca: our homage to that wonderful Spanish poet killed by the anti-Republican forces. To think that his books were burned in Granada, on the Plaza del Carmen ... Poor man!

We're planning the first number for the end of the year.

July 11, 1938

Back in Algiers after trips to Oran and Constantine. I've toured the country from one end to the other. Unfortunately, I didn't have the time or the means to cross the border and go to Tunis, where I would have liked to meet Armand Guibert, whose work I admire. He has achieved something quite unique, I think, with his magazine *Cahiers de Barbarie*.

July 13, 1938

I've managed to save a little and balance my budget, but the whole enterprise is fragile and could collapse at any moment.

July 15, 1938

Letter to Armand Guibert: "Would you be willing to entrust me with a manuscript: an essay or poetry, as you prefer? I would very much like to have something of yours in the 'Mediterranean' collection, if the idea is agreeable to you. Naturally all the review copies would be sent out according to your instructions; you would receive 45 author copies from a print run of 450, and retain copyright. The publication date would be in November or December."

July 18, 1938

Death of my maternal grandfather Joseph, Jean Salvator Nunziato Georges Grima, at the age of 82. Now that he has been struck down I feel a little more like an orphan.

September 19, 1938

After reading number two of the *Gazette des amis des livres*, I wrote to Adrienne Monnier to express my admiration for her book-store and tell her what an inspiration she has been to me and my friends in Algiers. I also passed on a news item that I thought would interest her: a nasty piece of fraud perpetrated by an unscrupulous bookseller. He would read the death notices and then send books to the mourning families, at exorbitant prices, claiming that they had been ordered by the deceased. What a racket!

I told her the story on my new letterhead. It's splendid, but maybe *Les Vraies Richesses* is printed in too large a font? I'll ask Fréminville or Camus.

November 3, 1938

It's the birthday of Les Vraies Richesses! We've made it through the first two years; we can last another twenty! I felt proud, looking over the catalogue of Éditions Charlot. Less so when I did the accounts. This work is leaving me no time for Manon, or my family, or my friends ... I spend my days reading manuscripts, trying to balance the books; then there are all the lunches and dinners, the visits to the printing works, and thousands of administrative obligations. It's exhausting and exciting at the same time.

December 17, 1938

Same thing again today: the customers were only interested in the latest prizewinners. I was trying to introduce them to new writers, recommending Camus's *Betwixt and Between*: not a flicker of curiosity. I'm talking literature, but they want bestsellers!

December 28, 1938

It's an uphill struggle, but the networks are growing, the friendships are there. Camus often drops by to lend a hand. He fills in the subscription cards, borrows books, or buys some when he has a bit of cash. He sits on the step or goes up to the mezzanine to write, read, or edit for me. He's at home here.

Yesterday I announced to him that I had sold the very last copy of his first book, *Betwixt and Between*. 350 copies.

January 18, 1939

A strange letter came from Grasset: they were intrigued to learn that a single store in Algiers had sold several hundred copies of Rilke's *Letters to a Young Poet*. It was the first they had heard of my obscure establishment.

January 31, 1939

Read a new text by Camus, beautifully entitled *Nuptials*. It captures our whole life here in Algeria. Deeply touched and moved. Because of the curious reticence that governs my friendship with Albert, I'll have to rein in my enthusiasm when I talk to him about it. I'm going to publish it in May, with a big print run: 1,225 copies.

February 9, 1939

My pal Max-Pol Fouchet helped me close the store, and we went for a drink: the classic anisette. He was telling me about his father, gassed at the front when he was trying to save wounded German soldiers; ten years later, on his deathbed, he made Max-Pol promise always "to extend the hand of friendship to the Germans." Then the waitress appeared, and my friend recited one of his poems to her. The young lady blushed with pleasure, won over by his enthusiasm, eloquence, and refinement. It's good to see him like that: handsome and charming. No longer brooding over Simone Hié, who left him to marry Camus, before cheating on *him* in turn. Friends are always falling out over women, but what could we do without them? Nothing!

March 17, 1939

Max-Pol Fouchet has joined the editorial team at Charles Autrand's magazine *Mithra* and renamed it *Fontaine*, in homage to the novel by the English writer Charles Morgan. He's asked me to be the publisher. We'll start at number three to maintain some kind of continuity with *Mithra*.

May 7, 1939

Went for a walk on Sunday with Jean Grenier, in the park up in Hydra, a residential neighborhood in the hills.

I'm happy.

July 22, 1939

Long discussion last night with Max-Pol Fouchet and Emmanuel Roblès. I confessed to my friends that I have never separated publishing from bookselling. Never. For me, it's the same thing. I can't see how you can be a publisher if you have no experience of bookselling. You might as well be selling breath mints. Afterward, it occurred to me that it's like a set of Russian dolls: Les Vraies Richesses, publishing, books, painting, friends ... All the same thing.

September 1939

I've been called up. I'm handing over the running of the store to Manon and any friends who are willing to help out.

October 1939

Advertisement in *L'Écho d'Alger*. Just two lines: *Les Vraies Richesses, 2b R. Charras. Lending library subscriptions, 5 to 7 pm.*

3

Ryad looks through the mail on the desk. He finds some red sticky labels, and amuses himself for a while making geometric patterns with them. He throws a bundle of postcards into the bin: lots are in black and white, and they look very old. He notices a date on one: 1950. After a moment's hesitation, he tosses it out along with the rest. There are some bills too, and numerous invitations to events of all kinds: openings, poetry readings, advance screenings. One is for a film about the first years of independence. Ryad saw it in Paris with Claire, in the Bastille neighborhood. They sat right at the back of the cinema. During the film, he whispered something in her ear, something silly, a bridge from mind to mind, a breach in the silence. Absorbed by what she was watching, Claire said nothing in reply. Ryad let her contemplate those images in black and white, those stories from the past. Eventually the lights came on again. Most of the people in the cinema were old, with doll-pink faces and white hair like sheep's wool. Some were crying, others seemed angry. Ryad took Claire briskly by the arm and led her out. She said something about the tragic fate of the characters. "Everything's always tragic in Algeria," Ryad replied. She laughed, thinking it was a joke. And they walked away through the streets of Paris, already deserted.

* * *

All these books are making Ryad anxious. He doesn't like words bunched together in a line or on a page; they unsettle him. Those black characters printed on white paper remind him of mites. His mother is terrified of mites: she scours the house with bleach from dawn till dusk. Do publishers and printers ever think about this? Are they aware of the risks associated with mite infestations? Do they even care? And do readers know what they're picking up and holding? They spend hours with their noses in a book and then they go to the pharmacy to complain about rashes, respiratory problems, blemishes, abrasions. And if the pharmacist has the nerve to recommend a break from reading, they're scandalized.

Night is falling. Ryad switches on the lights. All afternoon he has stared at the books. He imagines them falling on him. Claire once told him a story about a writer, Guibert something. He climbed up on a stepladder to get a book from a shelf at his house in the Tarn, and tripped. He grabbed at the shelves to steady himself and brought them down. He was found dead, buried under his books. Through the rain-spattered window, Ryad can see Abdallah, still standing on the sidewalk. Now and then, his face is contorted by a wince of sharp pain.

The young man gets back to work. He sweeps everything off the desk into a big rubbish bag: the mail, the invitations, the dirty old cup, the scissors, the felt-tip pens, the stapler, the tube of glue, even the red telephone with its severed cable. Then he takes the books off the shelves, starting from the bottom. His movements are slow and precise. He can't help glancing up at the image of Edmond Charlot. He has the strange and unpleasant impression that he is being watched; perhaps it's all those black-and-white photos of writers. He thinks about taking them down straightaway but then decides against it.

The books now form a multicolored monument on the floor.

There are slim and thick volumes, deluxe editions, picture books, cheap paperbacks, classics, old leather-bound tomes. He reads a few titles: *Nuptials*, Albert Camus, *The Roundness of Days*, Jean Giono, *The Heights of the City*, Emmanuel Roblès, *The King's Dance*, Mohammed Dib, *Earth and Blood*, Mouloud Feraoun, *The Circle of Reprisals*, Kateb Yacine ... When he drops a book back onto the pile, a poster folded in three slips out from between the pages. He scans it quickly:

Formerly Edmond Charlot's bookstore, Les Vraies Richesses. Membership applications must include 2 photos, 1 school certificate or certificate of employment, electricity bill or residency certificate, photocopy of identity card, fee of 300 dinars. Members may borrow 2 books at a time for a period of 15 days, renewable on request. Open: Saturday to Thursday, 8:30 am to 4:30 pm.

Biography of Edmond Charlot, bookseller, publisher, literary activist ... published the first books of Camus, Roy, Fouchet, Kessel, Roblès, Gide, García Lorca ... the Free French publisher during the Occupation ... In May 1936, under his initials E. C., Charlot published Revolt in Asturias, *a collectively written play based on a scenario by Albert Camus, banned by the Municipality of Algiers. Edmond Charlot opened his store on the 3rd of November ... with permission from Jean Giono to use the title of one of his books ... called up in September of the same year and stationed in Blida, he handed over the running of the store for 10 months, before returning in 1940 ... solitary confinement in the Barberousse prison, house arrest near Chlef ... the bombing of his other bookstore in 1961 and the destruction of his archives ... left Algeria for Paris at the end of 1962 ... returned to Algiers, and later worked in Turkey, Morocco ... Pézenas, near Montpellier, where he opened a bookstore ... lost his sight ... died in 2004.*

Making sure to keep Charlot's head visible, Ryad scrunches the poster into a ball. He takes aim at the gaping garbage bag, shoots, and cries "Goooaaaalll!"

On top of one of the bookcases, he finds a large red folder full of receipts, which ends up in the trash as well.

Darkness is settling over the street. Only the white sheet betrays the presence of the old man on the sidewalk: a light patch, floating as if unreal. Ryad is hungry. When he steps outside, the wind lashes his face; he heaves a weary sigh and goes to the pizzeria next door. Inside, the greasy walls shine; stuck to one of them is a photo of a soccer team. Moussa takes the orders, makes the pizzas, serves them, and works the till, all on his own. He is wearing a spotless blue smock with three pockets stuffed full of receipts. The customers are all men, standing, gobbling pizza squares. Mouths wide open, revealing broken, discolored, filled teeth. They chew the baked dough, the tomatoes, the industrial cheese.

Germany, 1940

Nazi journalists publish stories about the situation in the countries of North Africa, under French occupation. German radio even begins to broadcast in Arabic. We are stunned to hear these journalists calling on us, from Berlin, to take arms against France. It is said that in the middle of the night German soldiers are being parachuted into remote Algerian villages. They bring canned food and chocolates for the children. They have come to convince us to join Hitler's army, which will drive the French out of the country, they say: thanks to Germany, all our children will go to school, and Algeria will become a Muslim country again. Years later, we will discover machine guns and German helmets in those villages. Our grandparents will shrug their shoulders: "A young German soldier came down in a parachute ... He brought us food, so we hid him."

But France needs the natives for its army. "On the day of victory, the Mother Country will not forget all that she owes to her children in North Africa." We are the shoe shiners, the storekeepers, the sellers of fruit and vegetables who cultivate tiny plots of land, the keepers of goats and sheep. We are not yet adults. We have never really been children. We hate Europe: its factories swallow

our fathers and we see them come back broken by deprivation and
fatigue. We enlist in the army. They give us uniforms and spout
grand speeches at us. We become a little French, but not really.
Most of us are infantry, cannon fodder. We are obliged to fight for
a country that we don't really belong to. Over and over, we hear
the words *homeland, courage, honor* ... but the truth is, on the front,
it's hunger we think about, and the cold, and this war that makes
no sense to us, and the dead whose bodies we cover as best we can,
after reciting a few verses from the Koran. We memorize the date of
death, the place, and even the look of the surroundings so that we
will be able to tell it all to the widow or the mother or the child. We
pray to all our gods in all our languages. We fight for this country
as if it were ours. We smoke together when we have cigarettes, and
play dominoes between attacks. We are arrested, imprisoned, tortured, executed. When night comes, those of us who have survived
the hunger, the bombs, and the camps, having left our women and
children destitute in Algeria, repeat the promise fervently: "On the
day of victory, the Mother Country will not forget all that she owes
to her children in North Africa."

Edmond Charlot's Notebook
Algiers, 1940–1944

June 30, 1940

Met air force captain Jules Roy. A flamboyant, impulsive man; disconcertingly direct. Big reader.

July 10, 1940

Demobilized! I can take charge of my life again. But this damned war is complicating everything. Camus is living in the Haute-Loire. Hard to get manuscripts in and out.

September 3, 1940

Haven't been able to replenish my supply of paper for nearly four months.

September 22, 1940

Midnight. I can hear planes flying overhead. Happy to be publishing García Lorca's *Prologue*, after all the problems along the way. It won't be a very handsome edition. I can't be too fussy about paper, fonts, and layout in turbulent times like these. The main thing is getting it out. We do what we can and use the paper that people are willing to sell us.

October 30, 1940

The office of censorship ("Anastasie" as we call it) is wielding its scissors: they seized number three of the magazine *Rivages*, devoted to Federico García Lorca. They came to the store and destroyed every copy. Not a trace of our homage will remain. We're not giving up.

November 19, 1940

Hardly any books left in the store. To get paper, I have to scheme, beg, and shout. Our faithful customers keep coming for whatever they can find, which isn't much.

December 7, 1940

Letter to Emmanuel Roblès to reassure him about the publication of his *Paradise Valley*, which has been slightly delayed: "Now we just have to wait. Anastasie won't get to it until the final stage of the process." I'm already talking it up with journalists and readers, telling them the publication date.

January 3, 1941

Emmanuel is really very anxious. I owe him an explanation. Draft: "I'm having some serious problems with your *Valley*. First the printer, now the paper suppliers. I'm fuming, believe me, and the worst of it is, I'm already getting orders since the publication date has come and gone." Wretched books!

March 10, 1941

Camus has sent me a massive tome. Three texts that he sees as parts of a whole: *The Outsider*, *The Myth of Sisyphus*, and *Caligula*, under the general title *The Absurd*. Impressive work. My feeling is that these three are even better than what he's given me in the past. Should I publish them? I'd love to, but the way things are, it's impossible: out of paper, out of binding thread, I don't have a printer, and basically ... he needs someone in Paris with more substantial means.

March 13, 1941

I told Camus that I couldn't publish his new work and advised him to try Gallimard. This Occupation, it's like somebody holding your head under water, or a winter that goes on and on. How will it end?

March 19, 1941

My brother, Pierre, and Albert's brother, Lucien Camus, have joined the team at Les Vraies Richesses. They've taken over a large part of the administration: a great help to me.

June 7, 1941

The proofs of *Paradise Valley* are finally ready to be sent to Roblès for checking. I wrote and asked him to send them on to Camus, who will look after the publication. It's a weight off my mind.

August 1, 1941

Roblès's novel has been delayed again. *A Guide to Wartime Publishing*, that's the book I should write!

September 12, 1941

At last! *Paradise Valley* by Emmanuel Roblès in stock. Overjoyed.

December 14, 1941

A difficult end to the year, in every way, but we have some fine projects in the pipeline. Max-Pol Fouchet is more and more involved. We're working on *Paris France* by the American Gertrude Stein, full of wonderful anecdotes (very funny but also poetically told) about her childhood and her life in Paris.

February 4, 1942

Publication of *Three Prayers for Pilots* by Jules Roy, with a print run of 615 copies. It's a slim volume: a dozen unnumbered pages. The only paper I could find was heavy, unbleached, and rough, but the ever-faithful René-Jean Clot drew a beautiful portrait of Jules, which I put in as a frontispiece.

March 17, 1942

Just out of prison. A month inside! Thanks to Gertrude Stein who had the bright idea of declaring, in an interview with the BBC: "I have a very dynamic publisher in Algiers, who is resisting ..." Vichy already had me under surveillance. Three days after the book was printed, the police came for me in the small hours of the morning.

Very pleased with themselves, they declared: "By virtue of the authority vested in us, we hereby place under house arrest Monsieur Charlot, presumed Gaullist and communist sympathizer." Then they questioned me at length, asking me where Albert was. "Albert? Oh, but I must know a dozen Alberts. There's Albert the cobbler, for example: no one can patch up a sole the way he does. Or Albert the postman's son, bit of a drinking problem, but absolutely charming." "Stop playing the fool," they said, "and tell us where Albert Camus is." "Ah, Albert *Camus*! I don't know where he is. I truly don't know ..."

That was when they took me away and locked me up in the Barberousse prison, before putting me under house arrest at Charon, near Orléansville. In prison I met a craftsman from the Casbah who'd been arrested because of a vague resemblance to a safecracker. Maybe I'll write about him one day.

Camus is safely hidden in Oran. They're after Max-Pol Fouchet too; he managed to hide in the US consulate. I was freed thanks to the intervention of the journalist Marcel Sauvage, who used to manage a hotel in Tunis and is now the editor of the magazine *Tunisie-Algérie-Maroc*. He was able to influence the Minister of the Interior.

This unfortunate episode has held up the publication of Gertrude Stein's book, but the store stayed open, thanks to Manon and our friends. It's clearer than ever to me that without friendship there could be no Éditions Charlot. It all depends, essentially, on circumstances, friendships, and encounters.

April 1, 1942

The war has thrown everything into chaos. I can't get any more paper or ink. The results of my latest effort were pitiful: I had to staple the book because there's no more thread, and use dirty, porous butcher's paper.

April 6, 1942

A day of do-it-yourself chemistry with Max-Pol Fouchet. We bought some grape-seed oil on the black market at a scandalous price (I didn't dare tell Manon). Then we shut ourselves up in the kitchen and carefully mixed the oil with chimney soot and boot polish. What a sight we must have been, the pair of us peering into the big pan. The ink is yellowish, blackish, filthy. And the stench! I've never smelled anything so disgusting.

April 17, 1942

No more paper, no more binding thread, no more ink. Nothing. I wander around the city in search of any material that will enable me to go on publishing and printing. Leaves? Earth? Mud? I don't know what to do anymore.

May 18, 1942

A visit from the police: they came to Les Vraies Richesses to remind me that if I want to get paper, I have to submit the manuscripts to the Control Board first. Bastards.

May 22, 1942

I put an advertisement in the newspaper offering good prices for old and new books (first editions, rare titles, fine bindings, illustrated books). If I can't print, I have to get stock from somewhere.

June 6, 1942

Birth of Frédérique, our first child. Great joy. Manon is recovering gradually.

June 15, 1942

Wrote to Jules Roy warning him that I will have to send his *Sky and Earth* to the paper distribution committee: they'll decide whether or not it can be published.

July 2, 1942

Visited my printer Emmanuel Andreo. He's doing his best but the results are catastrophic. He warned me: "Your books won't last; this ink we're using eats into the paper from both sides ..." It also has a lingering, acrid smell. But what can I do? The only paper to be had is the bit that's left on the ends of the rolls from the rotary presses, the "steaks," as they say. There are holes all over the place. It gives a very poor impression of French publishing. One day, perhaps, someone will buy these books with Éditions Charlot on the cover, switch on a lamp, and open them up to discover white pages full of stinking holes.

September 5, 1942

I got in touch with Hachette; they laughed in my face: they have no stock. A distributor without books, it's unheard of. Unimaginable. We've run out of everything, I'm desperate. The shelves are almost bare. It looks so sad ... I have to plot and scheme to publish anything at all. When a new book comes onto the market, it sells out almost straightaway, but there's practically nothing left to print on. How am I going to survive?

September 11, 1942

The shelves are still bare. I'm keeping the store open every day because friends drop in to see me, and people come in off the street to talk. It has come to this: Les Vraies Richesses without books.

November 8, 1942

Spent the evening at Max-Pol Fouchet's; he insisted that I go. I must have looked like a bird of ill omen, wrapped in my black overcoat all night. There were lots of people. A great pleasure to see René-Jean Clot, and Frédéric Jacques Temple, a young soldier who has been in Algiers since the beginning of last summer; he writes, and has excellent taste in poetry. The Jewish singer Agnès Capri, who has taken refuge in Algiers, was there as well. The atmosphere was charged; people kept alluding to a mysterious event that was to take place in the course of the night. I went home around four in the morning, and an hour later, the Americans landed! Max-Pol had feared that we might be arrested, so he brought us all together for protection.

We're no longer under the control of Vichy. This is the capital of Free France!

November 12, 1942

I can't keep up with the requests and orders. Paper is available again.

November 21, 1942

Camus is stuck in Chambon-sur-Lignon, where he was convalescing. He was to return to Algeria by boat, but the American landing has left him stranded. His wife, Francine, who came back earlier, tells me that his financial situation is precarious. Unfortunately, I can't find a way to send him money; all communications are cut.

December 2, 1942

Called up again: assistant to Admiral Barjot in the provisional government, in charge of propaganda. I'm running the publications department in the Ministry of Information. We are planning to set up "France Publishing." A young colleague asked me why I don't write, since I love literature so much. I didn't dare tell him that writing bores me. What I like is publishing, collecting, sharing, bringing people together through the arts!

December 11, 1942

Dinner with Soupault, who told me the story of his journey across Tunisia on a bicycle. He managed to get away the day before the Germans took Tunis. Then he went back in an air force plane to get Gide. I'm glad to have met him. We had a long discussion about the possibility of launching a series together. Pocket editions for the five continents, published in five languages. An ambitious project (especially the way things are now), but it's exactly what we need!

December 17, 1942

I'm leading an odd sort of life: mostly I'm shut up in the barracks, but in the little leave I get, I'm meeting masses of people. Since the Americans landed, writers and artists, men and women from all over are arriving in Algiers. Strange times.

March 5, 1943

Dinner with Gide and Saint-Exupéry, who have both come to live in Algiers. Saint-Exupéry seemed depressed; the Americans are refusing to let him fly. He hid his frustration well enough not to spoil the meal, and played a fine game of chess with Gide. He also provided some entertainment: card tricks and prestidigitation. He had brought his one copy of *The Little Prince*, published in the United States. He refused to lend it to me and would only let me look at it sitting right beside him. It's a beautiful edition; the illustrations have come up splendidly. I tried to convince him to let me publish the book here, in Algiers, because I'm sure it would be a big success, but he refused. He's worried that it wouldn't match the quality of the US edition, and he's right; I don't have the means to do that kind of work.

Before I left, Gide took me aside to tell me about his project of launching a magazine to serve as a vehicle for the diffusion of

French thought around the world. He's worried about what's happening with the *Nouvelle Revue Française*, controlled by the Germans through Drieu La Rochelle, even if the publisher Jean Paulhan is doing what he can, with the support of Gaston Gallimard. Gide has already talked to the young poet Jean Amrouche, who is very enthusiastic and is planning to move to Algiers soon. I told Gide how much I admired the batch of Amrouche's poems that Guibert had sent me. Curious individual, Jean: Kabyle, Christian, French, Algerian background, teaching literature in Tunis. We could do something really good together.

April 3, 1943

Lots of traveling with the provisional government. Luckily Manon and our friends have been able to look after Les Vraies Richesses. At night, I'm working on manuscripts and this magazine we're trying to set up, Gide, Amrouche, and I. We have a name for it: *L'Arche*.

May 20, 1943

I've just heard that Drieu has resigned from the *NRF*. *L'Arche* is well placed to become *the* important French magazine after the war.

June 12, 1943

I'm signing a good number of French authors. The catalogue has never been so rich: Bernanos, Bosco, Giono, loyal as ever. I'm publishing foreign authors too: Austen, Moravia, Silone, Woolf.

June 27, 1943

The governor is courting the Muslims, promising them the moon. The powerful colonial families are furious. Who knows, maybe we'll have more justice in this country after the war.

June 30, 1943

Spent the whole evening reading a new manuscript from Gide: pages from his journal, 1939–1941. I was so overcome I offered him a 20 percent royalty. He refused; he wants 10 percent like everyone else, and told me that in any case he wouldn't sign a contract because that's not how he does things. I'll give him 15 percent.

July 11, 1943

Thanks to my pilot friends, our books are going to Lebanon, Egypt, and South America. Before they set off on a mission, they stop by Les Vraies Richesses to pick up bundles of books, which they sell on to stores at the other end. I'm an international publisher!

I'm also receiving a great many letters from Armand Guibert, who is living in Portugal now. He tells me that I absolutely have to get Fernando Pessoa translated and invited to France. And he always ends up complaining that I've forgotten him: "I am no longer in your thoughts ..." I like Armand a lot, but responding to all these long letters of his is taking an eternity. If I don't answer them quickly enough, he gets cross and bombards me with grievances. And his little ways can be trying: he expects a pretty stamp on every envelope.

September 27, 1943

Amrouche has approached the chief of the Information Division and asked for permission to publish *L'Arche*, plus a monthly paper allowance, and a one-time subsidy of 250,000 francs to help us launch our magazine.

October 7, 1943

Frédéric Jacques Temple entrusted me with ten of his poems. I gave him one of my personal copies of *Nuptials*. He's about to set off for Italy with General Juin's French Expeditionary Forces, and Camus's book will go with him. I'm keeping his work safe. Something should be done with it one day: they're very fine poems and deserve to be read. He promised he would write from the front.

October 19, 1943

I was notified by telephone that a package for me had come from

London in the diplomatic pouch. Inside there were photos of proofs: a text entitled *The Silence of the Sea*, and a penciled note: "Please reprint immediately." The author's name means nothing to me: Vercors. As far as I can tell, the text, which is fairly short—it's a long story or a novella—was published secretly by Minuit last year, then republished in July by Cahiers du silence in England. They're asking me to reprint, but that's all they say. Nothing about how many copies, or how they want it done (do I keep the author's name?).

How did they even know about me? Odd.

October 20, 1943

Started reading the Vercors and couldn't stop. I absolutely have to publish this. I showed it to my printer Emmanuel Andreo, who sat down and read it in front of me. Give me a day, he said.

October 21, 1943

Emmanuel has just left Les Vraies Richesses. He collected all the paper he could find, regardless of color and type. He has enough for 20,000 copies of *The Silence of the Sea*! It will be a multicolored edition on green, yellow, and pink paper ... but it will be readable! We're going to press straightaway.

October 31, 1943

The Silence of the Sea has sold out in a week: not one copy left in Algiers! The shelves are bare. Everyone's talking about it. They say the Free Forces are parachuting it into occupied France. Resistance!

November 6, 1943

Got the go-ahead for *L'Arche*. As well as Gide and Amrouche, we can count on the journalist Robert Aron. Lucie, Edgar Faure's wife, has agreed to let us use her apartment as our office.

January 30, 1944

Robert Aron told me that Gide doesn't want his name in the contract for *L'Arche*, although he's very keen to be part of the adventure.

He thinks we should take control of the project: the young should be in charge. Good!

February 2, 1944

The first number of *L'Arche* is about to go to press, with a text by Saint-Exupéry, which we're especially proud to publish: "Letter to a Hostage."

February 3, 1944

Robert Aron and Jean Amrouche are bombarding each other with letters. Aron's accusing Amrouche of not respecting him as editor and having set up a contract for *L'Arche* that's unfair to me. (I didn't ask for anything!) Amrouche doesn't want Aron to bring in Lucie Faure as a line editor.

February 8, 1944

Robert Aron passed on General de Gaulle's congratulations on the first number of *L'Arche*: he was shown the proofs.

February 10, 1944

Amrouche and Aron keep firing letters like missiles at each other. I'm expected to intervene.

February 15, 1944

L'Arche is a great success. We'll have to reprint. Amrouche is proud, as he should be; he's doing an excellent job with the magazine, toiling away tirelessly.

February 17, 1944

I've come under attack for *The Silence of the Sea*. The communists want my head; they're saying I published a fascist book. It's because of the character of the good German. They want me to be tried by a military court. First I was a presumed Gaullist and communist sympathizer, now I'm a fascist ... You can't win as a publisher.

February 18, 1944

We got a shipment of paper released from customs: two tons in big rolls for the next number of *L'Arche*.

February 21, 1944

Robert Aron wrote to our printers, threatening them. He is insisting that nothing be printed for *L'Arche* without his signature and that all documents relating to the magazine be delivered to him. This is too much. I've been warned that he's taking legal advice. Gide and I will have to sort this out. Amrouche will remain as editor; the position is his by right.

March 11, 1944

Sold the last copies of *Nuptials*. 1,225 in six years.

March 29, 1944

Received a batch of poems from F. J. Temple, written in his tank during odd moments of calm. They're resonating in me still, here, in the middle of the night. Even though he's fighting on the front line, he hasn't lost his capacity for wonder.

August 1, 1944

It looks as though Saint-Exupéry crashed. That's what I've been told, at least. Last seen on the radar near the coast of Provence. I ran into him a couple of days before he left. He was standing on the pavement, lost in thought. He told me that the Americans had finally granted him permission for a few flights, including a reconnaissance mission, but he knew that they thought he was too old to fly. I tried to comfort him, saying that the war was coming to an end, that we were going to win. His reply was strange: "Yes, we've won the war, but we've lost it all the same." And off he went, with that worried look still on his face.

August 3, 1944

It's no longer a rumor, what people have been saying the past few days ... Saint-Exupéry has been reported missing in action. One of my dearest memories of him: we were invited to lunch by a mutual friend. When I arrived, everyone was there, except for Antoine. We waited and waited and finally, getting worried, I looked out the window. He was sitting on the pavement, in the blinding sun, surrounded by a mass of children shrieking with joy. He was making them little planes from the foil wrappers of army-issue chocolate bars. He always carried a supply of those bars and offered them to the children he happened to meet on his way. The little planes went spinning up into the sky, and the children, faces smeared with chocolate, ran after them, trying to follow their flight, leaping to catch them ... Adieu, Antoine!

August 13, 1944

Drieu tried to kill himself, I'm told. Is the *NRF* dead and buried? What will become of Gallimard?

August 25, 1944

Paris is free! At last!

September 19, 1944

News from France in dribs and drabs, but it's always the same story: arrests and trials. They're trying to lock up writers and publishers suspected of collaborating with the occupying forces.

September 21, 1944

Planning to open a branch of Éditions Charlot in Paris. It's now or never. There's an opening, as Grenier would say.

November 5, 1944

The *NRF* has been banned because of its collaboration with the Germans. Paulhan's in charge of winding it up, and Amrouche is champing at the bit. He's setting obsessively high standards for

L'Arche, which absolutely must, he says, replace the *NRF*. He's preparing to leave Algiers and move the magazine's office to Paris.

December 1, 1944

Still in uniform, but I've been transferred to Paris. I'll be leaving my wife and children behind in Algiers. My brother Pierre will look after Les Vraies Richesses while I'm away.

4

Ryad is sweating on his mattress, breathing unevenly. It's early in the morning. A feeling of panic overcomes him. The silence of the store weighs heavily, and Claire seems very far away. He sits up, one hand raking his hair, the other fumbling for the switch of the bedside lamp. With the light on, he can see the mezzanine more clearly. He looks around, disturbed by the thought of discovering something unfamiliar. He puts on his sneakers, hurries down the steep stairs, stumbles, recovers his balance, and flings the door wide open, hoping to lose himself in the noise of the city. He is met straightaway by a cold gust of wind and a bucketful of dirty water thrown by the neighbor upstairs, who is mopping her balcony. She bursts out laughing and disappears inside before Ryad can protest.

Beside the door, a woman with a horsey face is sitting on a three-legged wooden stool. She has laid out bottles of fake perfume on a small red carpet. Only the finest brands: Dior, Saint Laurent, Chanel, Hermès ... She greets Ryad cheerfully, pointing at her merchandise:

"Perfume for men. The best in the city, you won't find another range like this. Take one, I'll give you a discount: three hundred dinars, reduced from three fifty. A special deal for a neighbor."

"Er ... No thanks."

"Go on, get one for your princess, then."

"I don't have a princess."

"A handsome boy like you? How is that possible?"

" ... "

"Ah! So get one for your prince."

"No, it's not that, I just don't need any perfume."

"Yes you do, you smell bad. Here, I'll give you a little squirt for free. Come on, come here. It's hard for me to get up because of my sciatica."

"No, really, I just wanted to step out for ..."

"Come on, come here, don't be shy."

Ffsscchhtt, ffsscchhtt. Citrus on his neck, hair, and torso. On the opposite sidewalk, Abdallah is smiling, propped on his stick. Ryad goes over and asks:

"Shall we get a coffee?"

"Yes."

"You do smell bad, you know."

"I know, I know ..."

The old man leads him through a labyrinth of streets. In spite of his age and his stick, he walks quickly. The storekeepers greet him as he goes by, with a gesture, a *Saha*, or a *Bonjour*.

They come to a plain little café. Three portraits of ex-presidents hang on the wall: Ahmed Ben Bella, Houari Boumediene, and Mohamed Boudiaf. The radio is on, but turned down very low: a quiet buzz. The light is harsh and white. You can see into the kitchen at the back, where women with headscarves are calmly at work, yawning. One, young and pretty, in a tight blouse, squeezes her breasts in front of another, who nods in approval.

A man with a trouble-ravaged face is sitting at the counter, crying quietly. Beside him is a woman with a guitar, who plays a few notes and quietly hums. She greets Abdallah with a little nod.

Ryad and Abdallah sit down at a table with a blue Formica top.

Abdallah is out of breath. What is it? Ryad wonders: a blocked artery, the beginning of a heart attack, panic, or just sadness? His noisy, rhythmic breathing makes a sound like breaking waves. Ryad remembers the vacation in Provence, with Claire. She wore a sky-blue bikini, the same color as her eyes. The same sky blue as the sweater that Abdallah is wearing now as he stares across the table.

"Not many people have eyes as dark as yours, do they? I mean, they're so dark, you can't even tell the iris from the pupil; it's kind of scary."

"You're not scared just because I have dark eyes."

"No, no ..."

"What are you going to do today?"

"Clean up."

"Clean up? You mean clean out."

"Up, out, whatever."

"What's left?"

"The top shelves."

"Where the Pléaide editions are."

"You seem to know the store well."

"I've spent a lot of time there."

"Do you like reading?"

"I used to work there. I filled in the subscription forms, kept them in order."

"Subscription forms?"

"Yes. It was a bookstore until the 1990s; then it was turned into a lending library. Are you sleeping on the mezzanine?"

"Yes ... And did many people use it?"

"No ... Five borrowers a month, at the most."

"Oh well, that's all right then."

"All right? You think it's all right to close it down because there weren't many borrowers?"

"Well ... yes."

"You're a fool. What are you going to do with the books?"

"The owner wants me to throw them out."

"Throw them out? You're not going to throw them out. Books? Do you realize what you're saying?"

"What else can I do?"

"Give them away, keep them, anything, but don't put books in the trash."

"Do you like reading?"

"No."

"So why are you worried about these books?"

"They're important to me."

"You can buy them on the internet, now, you know. You can get any book delivered anywhere. You can even read them online or on a tablet."

"Tsss, tssss!"

Abdallah drinks the last drops of his coffee and gets up. Ryad reaches into his pocket but the waiter stops him with a quick gesture.

"For you, it's free."

Ryad mumbles a hurried thank you and goes out after Abdallah, who is already heading back to the bookstore. When they get there, the woman with the horsey face is negotiating with two teenage girls.

"I'll give you a Dior J'adore and a Pure Poison for five hundred dinars. As a favor."

"But I'm telling you, we've only got four hundred. Give us a discount."

"You're ruining me, you know that? You realize I have five children to feed? My husband couldn't keep it in his pants, he ran off with a man, a little gigolo."

"I'm telling you, it's all we've got."

"All right, all right. Take them, take them, but come back and see me again!"

In a cabinet, Ryad finds a series of books printed on fine, almost transparent bible paper. He ventures to open one but closes it immediately, repelled by the tiny letters. He lights a cigarette and smokes it in the doorway. The rain begins again. Big, heavy drops falling almost lazily. Abdallah waves from the opposite sidewalk. The two men stand there, facing each other in silence.

Around midnight, Ryad is still among the books. He feels neither hunger nor fatigue. Eventually he climbs up to the mezzanine and stretches out in the darkness with his hands under his head. He hears car horns and the screeching of tires on asphalt. From time to time, headlights shine in through the front window of Les Vraies Richesses, like suns that are born and die within the space of a few seconds.

A sad-sounding woman's voice rises from the street. Ryad tries to hear the words of the song over the noise of the wind and the rain lashing at the store window. Something about an impossible love, a man who has gone far away. The voice gathers strength, trying to hold on to the man. You must prepare to forget the images of the past, the unmistakable signs, prepare to lose yourself in sadness. I don't believe in separations, thinks Ryad, pulling the blanket up over his face, tears welling up in him suddenly. He imagines Claire beside him, lying on her back, her stomach rising and falling gently as she breathes. He makes an imaginary space for her on the mattress and tries not to move, to keep her there a little longer. The voice outside launches into a new song, accompanied by a guitar. Another story about a woman with a broken heart. This time, the man loves someone else. Claire, the mattress, the bookstore, Ryad, eyes shut. The song. The guitar. The rain on the glass. There's a knock at the door.

It's Abdallah.

Ryad hurries to let him in.

"Is everything all right?"

The old man nods. His black eyes are moist. Ryad leads him to the chair and makes him sit down.

"I don't want to bother you."

"I wasn't doing anything special."

There he is, Abdallah, back inside 2b, with the white sheet around his shoulders. He looks like a magus, a strange apparition. This is his place: he scans the room, searching for memories. At the sight of the books on the floor, he turns pale. Ryad builds himself a pile to sit on. From outside comes the sound of two drivers arguing, and others honking angrily, held up by the drawn-out dispute.

From his pocket, Abdallah takes some old photos, folded into four. He passes them to Ryad, who handles them carefully. The first shows Abdallah, much younger, beside a woman holding a baby. They are in a living room; white cloths embroidered with flowers and fruit cover the furniture.

The second photo shows a little girl, sitting on the ground, intently reading an old book: *The Child and the River* by Henri Bosco, Éditions Charlot. In the third photo, Ryad sees a young woman in a wedding dress, arm in arm with a stern-looking man.

"The first photo, that's my wife holding my daughter when she was a few months old. In this one, she's reading one of her favorite books, here in the store. And the last one is her wedding day."

"She's very pretty."

The old man nods, and a proud smile flickers across his face. Ryad asks:

"Did you like working here?"

Abdallah thinks.

"Yes. These books kept me company every day for years. At first, I spent the evenings sorting them, putting on the call numbers, entering all the information in a register. For each one, I had to write down the name of the author, the title, the ISBN number, the key words. I would read a few pages so I could write the summary and answer questions from borrowers ... It's hard to explain what this place means to me. I haven't told many people this, but I didn't enjoy reading then, and I'm not sure I do now either; still, I like to be surrounded by books, although I came to reading late. Back in the days of the colony, the schools were for the French; there was nothing for us. I learned Arabic at the *zawiya*. And French, that was only after independence, thanks to my wife: she taught me. She never made fun of my ignorance. She was very patient; she took the time to get me started. But for years it was hard for me not to feel intimidated by the printed word. Maybe reading isn't natural for people like me. A book is something you touch and feel. You should be able to turn down the corner of a page, or put a book aside and pick it up again, or hide it under your pillow ... But I can't do that. Even now, whenever I see a book, I want to put it on a shelf."

He leans forward:

"I've read this one though, over and over. This is *Les Vraies Richesses* by Monsieur Giono. I wanted to understand why the store was named after this book. Listen, this is my favorite part: 'They were used to waiting for orders and being told how to live. Now they decided to live as they pleased, simply, not listening to anyone, and everything was lit up, truly, as when we find the match and the lamp, and the house is illuminated, and we know at last where to reach for what we need, as when the dawn lights up a larger dwelling, and a part of the world that had been smothered by night's mud, with its valleys, rivers, hills, and forests, is revealed in all its living joy.' That's what I felt when I came to work in this bookstore."

The guitar has stopped playing. The singer is silent.

Sétif, May 1945

On the day of victory, the Mother Country will not forget all that she owes to her children in North Africa. Facing enemy fire, under bombardment, we defended France against the enemy. We were there at the battle of Monte Cassino and the liberation of the southern cities; we fought in Italy, where hundreds of our brothers fell, and we had to abandon their bodies; we freed Alsace and marched on into Nazi Germany. The bombs and bullets did not distinguish between French and Arab.

Ben Bella, who will be the first president of Algeria, is decorated by de Gaulle in Italy, where Mohamed Boudiaf fought as well, and Krim Belkacem, and Larbi Ben M'hidi: the future heroes of the Algerian revolution. Our courage is universally applauded.

In Algeria, people are preparing to celebrate the Liberation. We want to take part in the great outpouring of joy, but also to remind the French of the promises made during the war.

In Sétif, the authorities allow us to celebrate the victory, as long as we don't mix with the Europeans. And as long as our assembly is not political. The bells ring out. Thousands of us gather in the streets. Joyously, our march sets off. We are joined by people from all the surrounding countryside. For the first time, in the middle of the crowd, the green-and-white flag with its red symbols appears. We raise banners demanding equality with the French, the release of our political prisoners, and the independence of Algeria. We encounter a policeman, who is swept up by the crowd. He draws his gun and fires. A young Arab scout carrying an Algerian flag falls to the ground. We cry out in panic. This is the beginning of the massacres. The socialist mayor of Sétif, a good man, tries to intervene, to stop the shooting. He is gunned down. Who fired? We will never know. All day and all night they shoot at us. And the following morning, the killing continues. For two weeks, violence rages. French people out on their own are shot. The army arrests and executes thousands of Arabs. Arms are distributed to French civilians, who search and destroy whole villages. Pavements run with blood. Corpses are dumped in wells. At Heliopolis, they fire up the lime kilns to dispose of the troublesome bodies.

The young Kateb Yacine is a student at the lycée in Sétif. The future author of *Nedjma* is just fifteen years old. When he hears about the massacres, he goes to join the demonstrators, in spite of his mother's protests. He is soon arrested and thrown into prison, where he will spend three months, fearing every day that he will be taken out and shot. His mother is told that he is dead. Here she is wandering the streets, searching for his body. She cries, she begs, she prays herself crazy. Her family is obliged to have her interned in a mental asylum. She will never be herself again.

Throughout the province of Constantine, the army organizes humiliating rituals: we are forced to kneel before the French flag and shout that we are dogs.

Finally, they are back in Algeria, the Arab soldiers, lauded and triumphant. They are proud: France's victory is theirs as well. They were feted in Europe along with their French comrades, and they have returned with the list of their friends who died in combat, with their stories about life in the regiment and card games by the fire. They arrive in their uniforms, medals pinned to their chests, full of hope for the future. We welcome them in our ruined villages and tell them about the massacres.

General de Gaulle sends Paul Tubert to investigate. He studied law and political science; he has served in Tunisia, Madagascar, Morocco, Albania, and Algeria. He arrives in Algiers on the nineteenth of May. He is kept there for a week. Visiting the province of Constantine is out of the question. He makes the best of the delay, meeting with various figures from both sides of the administration, French and Arab. People open up. They begin to tell him about the horrors. Finally, on the twenty-fifth of May, he reaches Sétif, but on that day a telegram from the Governor General's office in Algiers orders him to return to Paris. On the tenth of July 1945, he warns the National Assembly. The situation is critical. We must react very quickly, he says. *Time is short.* The National Assembly is ill at ease. No official action is taken.

The Second World War has just finished. We know that we will soon have to take arms, and that France cannot stay in Algeria. The future president Boumediene, who is thirteen years old, has witnessed the massacres. Later, he will say: "That day I grew old before my time. The adolescent I was became a man. That day everything changed. Our ancestors turned in their graves. And their children understood that they would have to arm themselves and fight in order to be free. No one can forget that day."

The man in charge of the repression, General Duval, declares: "I have given you peace for ten years. If France does nothing, it will start again, and worse, and there will probably be no stopping it." The man is clear-sighted.

The organization of the revolt by men and women all over the country will take nine years. Nine years of meeting in secret, forming networks, recruiting a tiny army. They will be joined by French supporters of the Algerian cause: the mathematician Maurice Audin, the worker Fernand Iveton, the poet Jean Sénac, the officer cadet Henri Maillot, the doctor Pierre Chaulet . . . They will be hunted down, tortured, condemned to death. Many of them will die before the proclamation of independence.

We don't know it yet, but soon the insurrection will begin in Algeria.

For now, our front doors are closed. Each family mourns its dead and disappeared.

Edmond Charlot's Notebook
Paris, 1945–1949

January 2, 1945

The army has assigned me to the Office of Information, where I report to Major Albert de Bailliencourt, a graduate of the École Polytechnique. Office on the Champs-Élysées. There's a table, a chair, and work for one person. The problem is, there are three of us! I have to do something to fill in the morning. If they have nothing to give me, I'm free to go out for a walk. So I'm visiting Paris, time on my hands, while my wife, my brother and my friends are looking after Les Vraies Richesses back in Algiers. Amrouche is here with me, working tirelessly to build up the circulation of *L'Arche*.

On the advice of Camus, I've taken a room at the Hôtel de la Minerve on the Rue de la Chaise, in the seventh. A pretty blonde, who looks like the actress Yvette Lebon, rings a great big cowbell whenever a visitor comes to see one of the residents. A terrible racket! That's Paris for you ...

January 12, 1945

Recruited a secretary: Madeleine Hidalgo. She's perfectly trilingual and extremely efficient. We're working in the hotel dining room, without heating. Madeleine keeps sneezing. Her hands are red; she can barely grip the pen.

January 21, 1945

I'm spending my days searching for a place within my (modest) means but big enough to house Éditions Charlot.

January 31, 1945

Camus introduced me to the book designer Pierre Faucheux. An interesting man. I invited him to think about some new covers for my collections.

February 11, 1945

We can't work properly at the hotel; it's too cold to concentrate. We've moved to the Café de Flore, where we stay after breakfast, like Sartre and Simone de Beauvoir, who have settled in on the other side of the room, and seem to have come here, as we have, for warmth, real coffee, and silence. Amrouche, Poncet, Gide, and I are preparing to open the Paris branch of Éditions Charlot.

February 13, 1945

A letter from Roblès declining my invitation to join us here at Éditions Charlot in Paris. He's frank about how hard it would be for him to work with Amrouche. He also has another project: he wants to launch a magazine, with the aim of "forging durable friendships beyond the immediate and pressing concerns of particular communities." The idea is to publish in three languages: French, Arabic, Berber.

February 18, 1945

Wrote to Vercors to ask him what he wants to do about the edition of *The Silence of the Sea* published in Algiers before the Liberation. Does he want to cede the rights entirely to Minuit? Along with the letter, I sent him a copy of the *Journal officiel*, in which the communists are calling him a fascist and demanding his head. I hope he finds it amusing.

February 27, 1945

Faucheux has suggested a new look for all the covers. He thinks it will make the books sell. He's right: we have to combine design and content.

March 18, 1945

When I got back to the hotel, Madame Glorifet handed me a letter left by a pastor: *I have been told that you are looking for premises. A member of my congregation, who was a prisoner of war, has returned in poor health and is looking to sell his property in the Rue de Verneuil. Would you be interested?*

March 20, 1945

Visited the property: it's run-down. Three rooms in a row: not sure how we'll organize ourselves. But the neighborhood suits us, and the main thing is, it's affordable. I'm going to buy it!

May 8, 1945

Victory Day for France, and the first day at number 8 Rue de Verneuil for Éditions Charlot.

May 15, 1945

The news from Algeria is horrific. What happened in Constantine? Whenever the subject comes up, the temperature rises, and it often ends in quarreling. No one can agree about what should be done in Algeria.

June 3, 1945

The Paris branch of Éditions Charlot is now a limited liability company. But I'm keeping Algiers as the head office; I'll go back and forth.

The roles and titles have been determined as follows:

Editorial director: Jean Amrouche.

Commercial manager: Charles Poncet.

Managing director: Edmond Charlot.

Armand Guibert, back in France after all his traveling in Portugal, Italy, and South Africa, will be responsible for international sales. He's very pleased to be with us again. I have offered them all shares in the company. Madeleine is still part of the team, of course, along with a new recruit, Dominique Aury, recommended to Amrouche by Jean Paulhan. She was on the paper allocation committee during the war, so she could have useful connections and she comes with the support of Paulhan, who seems to be very attached to her.

June 10, 1945

I put an envelope full of cash on the table. For all the gang to dip into according to their needs. I feel like their father.

June 22, 1945

Amrouche is completely obsessed by *L'Arche*. He keeps writing to Paulhan, asking him to throw his weight behind the magazine. Symbolically, it would be quite a coup: the ex-editor of the *NRF*. And he keeps writing to Gide to remind him that he's the magazine's patron. I've tried, in vain, to make him understand that we have to handle these men with care; we mustn't give the impression that we're desperate. I'm very fond of Amrouche, but I'm not sure that he hears what I'm saying.

June 29, 1945

Paper is scarce. Will this ever end? There's a regulation, but it's unfair! Quantities are allocated in accordance with prewar production, and anyone who wasn't operating here in France before the arrival of the Germans can take a walk. I'm told that Malraux himself had to step in to ensure that Minuit got a quota.

August 2, 1945

Leaving for a week in Algiers. The trips back and forth are wearing me out. I'm always having to patch things up, smooth ruffled feathers, raise morale, and I'm doing it all at a distance. Having a head office on one side of the Mediterranean and a branch on the other complicates everything.

August 29, 1945

Dinner with Jules Roy, Armand Guibert, and Jean Amrouche in a charming Parisian bistro. I was rather distracted, and it must have been obvious. Money worries stop me enjoying the time I spend with my friends. I sat there looking at the three of them, each so different and yet united by the same dreams.

September 5, 1945

Amrouche is full of grand ideas. When manuscripts come in from young writers, he reads them carefully, always on the lookout for something interesting, beautiful, publishable. He sends back long, encouraging letters, and in some cases even arranges a meeting ... He can be curt, but I know that he has the best interests of Éditions Charlot at heart.

September 15, 1945

We're trying to organize the business, but competition is fierce, and we're seen as exotic Algerian newcomers. Still, we're managing to publish twelve to fifteen books a month.

September 18, 1945

Amrouche has convinced me to print expensive, stylish catalogues to publicize our authors and our books. He also wants us to take out ads in the press. Camus is skeptical; he's advising me to tread warily: "Put on the brakes, start small."

September 21, 1945

Lunch at a little restaurant in the Rue des Canettes with Soupault, Amrouche, Roblès, Aury, Poncet, Sauvage, and Fréminville.

Interesting conversation with Soupault, who has no end of connections. Thanks to him, we've come to agreements with many writers and agents. I like and admire him very much, perhaps even more than Camus from a literary point of view.

October 9, 1945

We're living like penniless students, struggling to support our families; we have to fight on all fronts at once. I'm appalled by all the things we've neglected. Some of our writers have never signed a contract. And I'm trapped in a legal labyrinth. Nothing in Paris works as it did in Algiers: the legislation is different; taxes aren't paid in the same way, or royalties, or printers' fees, or overhead, or salaries, or even social security contributions.

November 1, 1945

Writing to the judges of literary prizes, one after another.

Working on a letter to journalists to present some of our forthcoming titles. I'll get Amrouche and Camus to read the draft and give me their advice.

November 29, 1945

I've been informed that Gide asked Paulhan if he wanted to bring *L'Arche* into the Gallimard fold, but apparently Gaston Gallimard found the last number "flat." He even used the word "ridiculous," so I'm told. Amrouche doesn't seem to have heard. I'm furious. I confided in Poncet, who's worried because there's a rumor afoot in Paris that Éditions Charlot is about to go bankrupt. We have to hold our course, and above all stay united.

December 10, 1945

The Farm Théotime won the Renaudot Prize! I'm so glad for

Henri Bosco, who thoroughly deserves it. He's a fine writer, a Mediterranean, steeped in sunlight, Provence, and poetry, and he has a good heart! What a joy for him and Éditions Charlot, for everyone involved in this adventure. Up all night with my friends celebrating the news.

December 17, 1945

Man's Work by Emmanuel Roblès won the People's Novel Prize! How can I describe what I feel? All this frenzy around the prizes. It's as if the whole world were watching us. Absolutely overjoyed!

December 19, 1945

A letter came from Armand Guibert, dated November 26. I wonder where it's been in all this time. He has written a beautiful note about *The Farm Théotime*, which I'll pass on to Henri. He'll be touched.

January 17, 1946

Snowed under: New Year's greetings to reply to, letters of all kinds, orders from bookstores and other paperwork. My friends and family are paying the price.

February 5, 1946

We're publishing *On My Horse*, a collection of poems by Frédéric Jacques Temple. I haven't forgotten the promise I made to him before he left for the front. He wrote me a long letter to tell me how moved he is. Although I don't know him all that well, I feel that the friendship between us is deep. *One day I will set off to find you on my horse, without a saddlebag or a gun ...*

February 11, 1946

Letter to Guibert to remind him that Amrouche is still waiting for his contribution, and to say that I'd be interested in publishing something about Pretoria. I'm curious about the lives, the loves, the dreams of people there. Pretoria: what a beautiful name!

February 22, 1946

Reply from Guibert reminding me that I still owe him 17,430 francs, his salary for May, and the same for June, plus a fee of 38,000 francs for the translation of Ferreira de Castro's *Eternidade*.

February 27, 1946

I saw in the paper that Momo, my friend from the Casbah, had broken the world distance record for swimming underwater, in Paris. The man is incredible! A phenomenon! I kept the cutting.

March 6, 1946

We're facing enormous difficulties. The big publishers have recovered easily from the war, and competition is fierce. They look down on us; to them, we're Algerian interlopers, *hicks*. They're approaching my authors, I know, courting them, inviting them to dinner. They're promising the moon, saying I'll go bankrupt in a few months.

March 8, 1946

Paulhan has refused to join the editorial committee of *L'Arche*. Well, that's clear now, at least. Amrouche is furious and gloomy. All the obstacles (lack of paper, people failing to deliver, our competitors' dirty tricks) are wearing us out and preventing us from meeting our deadlines.

March 15, 1946

Publishing a book by Paul Tubert. The title is ironic through and through: *Algeria Will Be French and Happy*. Last year, General Tubert was commissioned by de Gaulle to investigate the Sétif massacres. He has offered me the text of his speech at the National Assembly. We agreed to date it July 10, 1943, before the massacres, to avoid any problems. And in order to reduce the risks for our printers, the colophon will read Special Press, which doesn't exist, of course. Sleight of hand, subterfuge.

May 2, 1946
Books and manuscripts piling up everywhere. We've run out of space. We have to find new premises, urgently. But we can't afford what we really need.

May 6, 1946
Amrouche has been on at me for weeks about an antique chess board he has found; he wants it as a gift for Gide. In the end I caved in and let him have the money. The things you have to do as a publisher these days.

May 22, 1946
It really is a strange life here, with the children and Manon back in Algiers. Publishing has ruled my life; it will end up costing me my family.

June 15, 1946
A quarrel between Amrouche and Poncet; they just don't get on, it's obvious. People tell me to watch Amrouche; they say he wants to run the magazine on his own (he already does). He's always demanding more respect, and so is Poncet. Childish, really.

October 29, 1946
Vincent Auriol summoned me to the Senate and asked me to reprint his book *Yesterday ... Tomorrow*. I told him I'm out of paper and don't even have a telephone. I'm out of everything, to tell the truth. "Just go ahead," he said, "you'll have what you need." Almost as soon as I got back to the Rue de Verneuil, the men turned up to install the telephone. We're sending Auriol's book to the printer now, for a run of 35,000 copies.

December 4, 1946

Jules Roy is celebrating his Renaudot Prize for *The Happy Valley*! He created a sensation by turning up at the office in his flying gear to sign copies of the book.

December 6, 1946

Visited the Crété printing works, founded in 1829 at Corbeil. They produce a good share of the books in our catalogue. Very impressed by the professionalism of all the employees.

December 22, 1946

The paper Auriol promised was never delivered. I'll just have to wear it. If he's elected president, his book will sell out in a few weeks.

December 31, 1946

Totting up today: almost 70 books published this year!

January 17, 1947

Auriol was elected yesterday, but the 35,000 copies of his book won't sell: there's a new law prohibiting publicity for a book by the head of state.

January 23, 1947

Lunch with Paulhan and Amrouche. Felt oddly superfluous. Endless problems.

January 24, 1947

Interminable meeting yesterday at the book industry cooperative. I'm trying to hold on, but our figures don't look good. If we want to get things back on track, we need more space so that we can organize our activities properly.

January 30, 1947

I urgently need to find new premises; we're much too crowded here and our projects are multiplying rapidly. The only way to get a decent space without paying a fortune is to buy a brothel. They're all for sale since the Marthe Richard law was passed a few months ago, outlawing organized prostitution and procuring. Which is why I'm touring the brothels, looking for a good deal.

February 5, 1947

The bookstores are ordering by telegram, and by the kilo, but we're still short of paper and I can't find any way to get more. Maddening. Victims of our own success. I need less success or more paper, and above all better financial support. Sales are reaching 100,000, and much more for some titles. *The Farm Théotime* will make it to 300,000, for sure. But the more good books we publish, the worse off we are financially. I've gone from being a small specialist publisher to a business drowning in orders ... and debts. I can't sleep.

February 9, 1947

A meeting at the bank, which didn't go well. In spite of the prizes and the publicity. The man I was talking to knows nothing about books and won't lift a finger to help me.

February 16, 1947

Still just as hard to get paper. I had to buy some on the black market at an exorbitant price. I sign what they put in front of me. Without being able to negotiate the rates or the delivery date. Am I doomed to spend my whole life chasing after paper?

February 21, 1947

Difficult conversation with Amrouche. I might be wrong, but I have the impression that he doesn't trust me.

February 25, 1947

Every day, every night, I hear of some hostile maneuver on the part of our competitors. They would love to send us back to

Algiers. They're courting our authors, bullying our suppliers. I'm no match for them. The Parisian publishers have money, paper, and connections. What do we have? Writers—the best—and commitment, but that won't be enough. We're a long way from 2b Rue Charras, and the bistros of Algiers, and our friends. We have no choice but to hold things over, beg the printers to rearrange their schedules, and warn people that payments will be delayed. Night after night I go over the accounts. I'm losing heart. Nothing is working out.

February 28, 1947

Ran into Gide who was wearing a dark red suit. That's how he gets his royalties from the USSR, he explained. His books sell well there, but he's not allowed to take the rubles out of the country, so they compensated him with bolts and bolts of fabric, which he had made up into a large collection of suits. I told Amrouche the story, but he seemed bitter. He feels that he doesn't have a real place in Gide's life; Gide never thinks of him ... I tried to explain that it's not like that, being a publisher.

April 8, 1947

Things are getting even worse. Amrouche says we'll have to take measures in the next five or six weeks in order to secure new funds. But what measures? And most of all: what funds? We can't pay our authors (Grenier in particular for his articles in *L'Arche*, to my great shame).

April 12, 1947

I have just sold my little property to a lady by the name of Marie Marquet, who will use it to sell opalines. Éditions Charlot is moving to an ex-brothel in the Rue Grégoire de Tours, famous for having been frequented by the poet Guillaume Apollinaire. We have bought the whole building, whose owner, they tell me, was murdered (which brought down the price). A brothel. A poet. A murder. If all that doesn't help us get back on our feet!

May 3, 1947

I sold Les Vraies Richesses to my brother Pierre: I couldn't take care of it any longer, and I needed the money to finish the work on my "brothel." It's costing more than I planned. Felt a pang when I thought of my little store at 2b Rue Charras: that book-lined corridor. But it's in good hands with Pierre and his wife.

May 7, 1947

News from Roblès, who has gone back to live in Algeria. He's launching a magazine, to be called *Forge*.

Long may it live!

September 12, 1947

An avalanche of expenses that I'm barely able to cover: lunches, catalogues that cost a fortune, but how could I do without them? I just can't find a solution, and the mood is grim in spite of our new premises.

January 28, 1948

We can't print anymore, not a cent left. I haven't been able to raise capital, and no bank will give me a loan.

February 17, 1948

Amrouche showed me the most recent letter from Jules Roy. He feels that we're not doing enough for him: his book is selling itself, without a publicity push from us, and he's not sure that he's with the right publisher.

March 19, 1948

Amrouche is searching for money: a patron, businessmen, bankers ... In vain.

March 30, 1948

Jules Roy has called in the lawyers to get out of all of his contracts with Éditions Charlot and move to Gallimard.

June 16, 1948

Camus has informed me that he's pulling out. He wants his royalties. I understand.

June 19, 1948

Amrouche has approached the multimillionaire Florence Gould (to whom he was introduced by Paulhan) and asked her for help to the tune of three million francs.

June 20, 1948

Got the cover for the new novel by Emmanuel Roblès, *The Heights of the City*. It was designed by a Tunisian artist, El Mekki. He came up with a green title against a dark background and a triangular fan of light, shining down on the city behind. It's somber and beautiful. Perfect for the novel, with its solitary hero, Smaïl. I had a rather ambitious idea, but I think it might pay off: extending the jacket and using the extra space to present the book. There could be back and front flaps, with a synopsis to encourage readers to buy it, as well as a biography of Roblès. It would be a first in French publishing.

August 5, 1948

Charles Poncet tells me that Guibert has agreed to settle for 26,000 francs instead of the 38,000 we owed him.

August 12, 1948

The shareholders of Éditions Charlot—my friends, that is—got together. They're demanding my resignation; they're willing to keep me on but only as a literary adviser. Charles Poncet and I will have to stand down. From a company that has my name. Éditions Charlot without Charlot. How is that possible? Twenty-two million in the red. It makes my head spin. Amrouche is in charge of the liquidation; people will have to be laid off, hard news to break. I'll have to sell everything I own, which isn't much, to pay my debts. I tried to comfort Dominique Aury and Madeleine Hidalgo, who seemed very downcast.

September 2, 1948

Amrouche and Autrand are taking over. Charlot's Band, as Jules Roy used to call it, is breaking up. Gallimard, Le Seuil, and Julliard are picking up most of my authors.

Back to Algiers, just me and my dreams of Mediterranean literature and friendship.

October 15, 1948

From Algiers, I sent Amrouche a beautiful manuscript by a poet from Oran. A curt letter in reply, reminding me of the situation Éditions Charlot is facing, the company's financial woes, the number of contracts that haven't been honored. He wants me to "reject immediately all manuscripts submitted in Algiers, even if they are masterpieces, rather than sending them on. It will save us time and postage." What happened to friendship? Where is it now?

I've heard that Florence Gould gave him 250,000 francs for *L'Arche* and now she wants the money back. He's claiming it was a gift, not a loan. He's trying to convince Gallimard to take on *L'Arche*, but it's futile. Gaston Gallimard is hoping to relaunch the *NRF*, and Gide seems to want to reconcile everyone. As for Paulhan, I don't think he understands Amrouche's rebellious attitude to France: he sees it as driven by resentment; that's why he's so wary.

November 29, 1948

Telegram to Roblès at his house in Bouzaréah: "Femina Prize for *Lights* [*sic*] *of the City*. Bravo. Very best wishes. Come back soon." I'm thrilled about this prize, in spite of everything.

January 10, 1949

They have included my cover copy in the design for the new edition of Roblès's novel. So there will be a synopsis and a biography of the author. It's a novelty, the talk of the publishing world.

March 8, 1949

Pierre is managing Les Vraies Richesses wonderfully, with the help of his wife. I have to start up something new. Sénac, the poet, back in Algiers after various adventures in France, is encouraging me.

May 22, 1949

New bookstore called "Rivages" at 18 Rue Michelet, with my uncle Albert. I have a thousand ideas already for how to put some life into the place. All fired up, in my shorts and espadrilles. Planning to make a gallery space in the basement of the store.

December 1, 1949

Éditions Charlot has been declared bankrupt by the commercial court. Our ill-fated Parisian adventure. As a group of friends, we failed.

Brutal end to a chapter in my life.

5

Ryad is preparing to lock up the bookstore when Moussa, who runs the pizzeria, comes over to invite him to dinner.

"My wife has made a good big pot of couscous, and Abdallah has been telling us all about you; we'd like to get to know you too."

The two men walk through the pizzeria, then down a long corridor where boxes of soft drinks are piled up along with cleaning equipment (a broom, a bottle of bleach, pink-and-white striped cloths, a drum full of water), before reaching a staircase that leads up to a dining room. Moussa gestures to his guest to take a seat.

"My wife and daughter are coming. Abdallah is praying, he won't be long."

The round table is covered with a fine cloth. In the middle sits an imposingly large dish full of couscous. Embarrassed, Ryad breaks the silence somewhat awkwardly:

"I'd like to thank you for inviting me to dinner."

"I'm happy to have you as our guest."

"Does Abdallah live with you?"

"Yes, he sleeps on the ground floor. He's a good man, you know."

"Yes ..."

"Has he told you about his life?"

"A bit."

"He's not the sort of man who opens up easily. That bookstore has quite a story, you know. I've always lived in this neighborhood, and I used to chat with the woman who owned it in the old days: Madame Charlot, we called her. A stocky little woman, who bought and sold secondhand books. When curious visitors came to her little store, she'd tell them how Camus used to work there, editing manuscripts, and talk about the exhibitions, and the writers. I thought she was the publisher's widow. Actually, she was the widow of one of his brothers. The poor woman left in 1992, when things started getting difficult here. You would have been just a kid then; it must seem like ages ago to you. Strange times, the 1990s. We didn't really understand what was happening. The news on the Algerian channel kept showing us the latest president, the army winning battles, people shaking hands. Do you remember? But life just kept getting harder. Shortages of everything. My wife stopped giving me shopping lists. I'd go to the market, buy what I could find, and as long as I got home alive, she was happy. One thing about terrorism, it keeps the women quiet. We thought it would all be sorted out quickly, but no. Those monsters would turn up in a village and kill men, women, and children. The next day, or the day after, we'd find out about the atrocities in the paper; that was the best source of information. Imagine the courage it must have taken to be a journalist then. They had to face it all: assassinations, bombs, threats, kidnapping, exile, abuse . . . But every day they turned up and went on doing their job. It really mattered to people like us, who had no other way of understanding what was going on. Sometimes I thought about writing to the journalists whose work I admired but I never dared, and now the time has passed. I'm talking too much."

"No, no."

"You're polite. Anyway, Abdallah's daughter used to come and visit him over the school vacations. The rest of the time, she was in Kabylia with her grandparents. The doctors said it would be best for her to move away from the city after her mother's death. She was a very shy little girl, hardly ever smiled. She'd stay up on the mezzanine, sitting on the floor and reading. She smiled then. Charlot left something beautiful here, something bigger than everything that was going on outside."

Ryad is sitting very still. Men don't cry, he knows that, but he can clearly see the tears in Moussa's eyes. His host takes a deep breath and goes on:

"Abdallah told me one day that writers, or at least the things they can imagine, had been a help to his daughter."

Moussa's wife comes in. Gentle face, laughing eyes. She smiles at Ryad mischievously. He recognizes the woman who doused him with a bucketful of dirty water. She is followed by a little girl who looks as if she just fell out of bed: her curly hair is all over the place. Ryad notices that she has the same birthmark as her father, in the shape of Africa. Mickey Mouse winks on her pajama top. Abdallah comes in after her, looking tired, clasping his prayer beads in his right hand. To go with the couscous, the mistress of the house brings a big *kesra* salad, a dish of meat, and another of chickpeas. *Bismillah.* In the middle of the meal, the little girl tells her father that she really *really* wants to go on vacation. Moussa snaps:

"We live right by the sea; this is our vacation house all year round."

Ryad smiles at the girl.

"I have some books for you in the store, if you'd like."

"No. I don't like reading. I like drawing."

Abdallah glowers at her. She adds:

"But there's a boy in my class who loves reading. He doesn't have any books at his place. Maybe you could give them to him?"

"OK, I'll try to take some to your school."

"Do you know where it is?"

Abdallah breaks in:

"We'll go for a walk after dinner; I'll show him."

Ryad follows the old bookseller, who leads him down dark alleyways. They stop in front of an entrance without any identifying sign. A man half opens the door and looks out warily. At the sight of Abdallah, a smile lights up his face. The man invites them in. They cross a little courtyard and enter a building with a cracked façade. In the basement, the walls are dark gray, as if charred. They pass overflowing trash bins, growling, skeletal cats, a slew of history books with torn covers, a broken flat-screen television, and a legless chair before reaching an immense, smoke-filled cellar. It's hard to guess how many people there are, the smoke is so thick and the lighting so subdued. A woman wearing thick makeup is talking on her cell phone in front of the door.

"I love you. Yes I do. Stop it, I love you."

Ryad leans over to Abdallah and asks:

"Where are we?"

"At Saïd's place."

"Saïd's place?"

"Yes, some nights, he opens it up."

"But what is it? A gambling den? A bar?"

"No, no, just a place where people can smoke and talk. Saïd can't keep the café open all night, he doesn't have the license, and everything's gotten so complicated here. Just to get together, you need a thousand authorizations. It's the age of bureaucracy and suspicion. So he runs it in secret, for regulars only. Have a look around, talk to some people your age. I'm going to bother the lawyers over there."

Ryad hesitates, not daring to approach any of the tables, and ends up sitting on his own, near a group of women who must be around thirty. They are accompanied by a much older man, with blond hair, wearing small dark glasses. Twenty books or so are piled on the table in front of the women. One after the other, they give the man a book and he says something that makes them laugh and clap. Noticing Ryad's curious gaze, one of them turns and speaks to him:

"I bet you're wondering what Youcef is doing to get us so excited?"

"Well, yes."

"Youcef is blind but he can recognize any of these books by the feel of the cover, and recite a passage from memory. You want to try and stump him?"

"OK."

Ryad slips one of the books into Youcef's hands: *The Farm Théotime* by Henri Bosco. On the handsome white cover, with its classic design, the letters NRF stand out in red. Youcef caresses the book, turns it over and around, smells it, and murmurs:

"In August, in our country, a little before evening, the fields glow with a powerful heat. The best thing to do is to stay at home, deep in the shade, waiting for dinnertime."

The women clap again. Ryad concedes defeat. He looks for Abdallah but can't find him, and ends up going home alone. The streets are dim, barely lit by a few lamps and the weak glow of the moon.

Algiers by night.

Algeria, 1954

On the tenth of October, in the working-class neighborhood of Bab-El-Oued, six men gather. Some months earlier, a motion in favor of armed revolution was carried at a secret meeting. The night of the thirty-first of October and the first of November has been chosen to mark the beginning of the insurrection.

On Sunday the twenty-fourth of October, the six edit the tract that will be dispatched from Cairo to foreign newspapers. Their resources are meager: only a thousand men, scattered around the country, with little combat experience for the most part. No money. A few hundred weapons. And, most of all, a population that they must convince in any way they can. After the meeting, they go down the street toward the Pélissier barracks, not far from the Majestic cinema, and enter a photographer's studio. There, they prepare themselves for the occasion, trying to tidy their curly hair, checking their ties.

There are only two stools. They consider the problem, the photographer offers his advice, and finally Krim Belkacem and Larbi Ben M'hidi sit down in front of Rabah Bitat, Mostefa Ben Boulaïd, Didouche Mourad, and Mohamed Boudiaf. "Hold still now." Click.

They don't know that this photo will be seen all around the world, that half a century later it will be shown to children at school.

At the same time, Jean Vaujour, Director of Security, is cursing his superiors who refuse to give any credit to the alerts that he keeps sending them. He's on edge. Something is brewing. But back in France they think that the 1945 massacres have killed any thought of revolt in the Arab population. Ho Chi Minh's army has inflicted a terrible defeat on the French at Diên Biên Phu. More than ever, France needs peace and quiet in its Algerian colony.

At 1:15 a.m., throughout Algeria, official buildings are attacked. There are ten fatalities, including four soldiers. A proclamation is sent to various capitals, demanding the withdrawal of the French. On the morning of the first of November, the weather is icy cold. Barely awake, we hear the news of the previous night's events on the radio. The sky, the light, the faces in the street: everything is white. In a single night, Algeria is drained of color. There is no other way to describe our country. Even the sun is white.

Suddenly, utterly, everything is changed.

Now we are fanatics, ingrates, puppets of foreign powers. Our attacks are cowardly, and we are unworthy of France. Young men are pulled from their beds half naked and taken away in police cars. No more half measures. A curfew is imposed. We are all under threat, under surveillance. Brawls break out: punches and headbutting. We no longer play cards in the cafés at night. The beignet vendors look down when the soldiers go past. The French Algerian ultras distribute tract after tract. Threats and strikes everywhere. These are the days of stares that brim with hate and fear, frustration and anger. A thick blend that envelops and engulfs us.

We will never sleep in peace again.

Edmond Charlot's Notebook
Algiers, 1959–1960

October 8, 1959

Tense atmosphere in Algiers. Jules Roy announced that he was in favor of Algerian independence, and the ultras have put a price on his head. The FLN has a delegation in New York now. There's something very moving about the way those young Algerians have persisted for three years, repeatedly raising the question of independence at the United Nations.

When the Arab storekeepers all went on strike two years ago, they sent in the army and forced them to open their stores. People haven't forgotten that, or the hijacking of the plane that belonged to the King of Morocco, with five leaders of the FLN on board. There are more and more stories about horrific acts of torture committed by the army. All around the world, people are calling for France to end this terrible war, because that's what it is, even if all the official statements refer to the "events."

October 12, 1959

Dinner with Mouloud Feraoun. I was scolding him for not having given me a chance to publish his novel *Poor Man's Son*. He smiled and told me, in that gentle voice of his, that he had sent me a copy in 1945.

On April 6, he still remembers, he received a letter from Éditions Charlot. He tore it open excitedly, but it was a simple acknowledgement of receipt. He waited patiently, as requested, didn't dare tell anyone or dream of being published one day: Mouloud, the little Kabyle who had learned to read almost by miracle. Eventually, in August, on the 6th once again, he received another letter on the Charlot stationery. He showed it to me. Such a cold, impersonal letter, saying no, mentioning an editorial committee, which had not selected his novel. It's an insult to a book so full of tenderness and generosity, a poignant homage to childhood. Jean Amrouche never mentioned it to me. Was it an oversight? Or jealousy? I'm appalled. Mouloud self-published *Poor Man's Son*, before being taken up by Le Seuil, thanks to Roblès. He told me that his book had been shortlisted for the Algerian Literature Prize, but although the members of the jury were full of praise for his work, they couldn't bring themselves to give it to a North African. They offered him a sum of several thousand francs as an encouragement, but he never received the money.

October 14, 1959
This business with Amrouche and Feraoun is still bothering me. Will I ever know what really happened?

January 4, 1960
Camus!

January 5, 1960
I was at a ceremony for an art prize when I got the call. I don't know who it was on the other end ... she was crying and saying over and over, "He's dead." It took me at least five minutes to understand who she was talking about.

January 19, 1960
Death of my maternal grandmother, the last real link with my mother. She died in Birmandreis at the age of 96. What a sad month it has been.

April 9, 1960

Terror everywhere. The official recommendations in the newspaper tell us to stay at home, but we have to work. How do they suppose we'll earn our living?

April 11, 1960

Heated discussion in a café yesterday. The kind that starts among strangers at a counter. I said: "I think it's scandalous and monstrous to go murdering civilians, planting bombs under streetlamps, killing cleaners and postmen, simply because they're Arabs." My friends are telling me to be careful. But careful of what, of whom?

April 17, 1960

I've noticed more and more young people coming to this store, but also the one at 2b, who simply can't afford to buy books. When I can, I slip them something I love and say: "Take it, pay me later." And a few weeks or a few months later, they come back with the money.

June 7, 1960

Yesterday, a young man, twenty years old, came to me with a manuscript. He could barely bring himself to look me in the eye. He has written beautifully about the lives of people here.

Idea for a magazine. Discussed it with Roblès, who's willing to come on board. I've got financing for six numbers, at least! We'll start in October, the whole group of friends. First number in January 1961: homage to Camus. Roblès has suggested a list of writers from Le Seuil who might contribute.

September 9, 1960

More attacks. The ultras issuing threats. Swine.

September 11, 1960

You'd have to be crazy to try launching a magazine in these circumstances. But if we don't do it now, it will be too late.

September 24, 1960

I was shown a tract that has been distributed to the young Algerian conscripts. There will always be paper for printing trash, that's the problem.

When our first soldiers came ashore in 1830, they did not find a nation, a sovereign, a government, a people, but tribes without defined territories, constantly at war with one another. The country was in a state of total anarchy. Nomads looted the villages. The cities bled the country dry. There was only one law: Might is right.

[...] And then, there is the future, your future. The reserves of oil buried under the sands of southern Algeria will yield, on estimate, 60 million tons per year—four times France's annual consumption—and in the far reaches of the Algerian Sahara, there is iron, copper, manganese, and the world's largest phosphate deposit.

October 6, 1960

For months, my customers have been asking me why I'm still here, what my plans are, where I will go. I'm staying; this is where I belong, and anyway, what would I do if I went somewhere else?

October 9, 1960

The banks are panicking because of all the transfers to French accounts. I can't print anything. The project for the magazine is on hold.

October 17, 1960

I've heard that some of the people who signed the Manifesto of the 121 have been censored or barred from all state funding. Vercors refused the Legion of Honor to protest torture in Algeria. The future of this country is tearing whole families apart.

6

The first morning with Claire. The room was freezing. When she pulled up the quilt he saw her fingernails painted sky blue. He had watched her writing words and sentences in a notebook with a red leather cover, and secretly hoped she was writing about him. "It's for me; stories from the past," she had said with a smile.

Claire is beautiful. A slim young woman with cold blue eyes. The problem with the color blue is the way it draws you in. You drown in it. You lose yourself.

She often mumbles in her sleep but says it's nothing, a bad dream, a cloud passing over, drifting by. She counts sheep and falls asleep again, smiling.

In the street, she walks quickly, glancing back from time to time, and always feels she's being followed. Sometimes, on the way home, the stares even make her want to break into a run. She laughs at her own fear, and turns it into an eccentricity. One day Ryad found her curled up on the sofa. He took her hand. It was warm, soft, slightly dry. Claire sat up. "I like it here, in this brand-new apartment that already smells old. I like being with you, and what we have, however fragile it is."

Ryad is impatient. He wants to finish this pseudointernship as soon as he can and get back to Paris to be with Claire. He can already see himself arriving at the apartment, finding her asleep in the double bed, slipping in beside her. She will make a grumbling noise and put her arm around him, kiss his neck.

Through the front window of Les Vraies Richesses, he sees drifting clouds reflected in puddles. This city is grim when it rains. Only a few sparrows break the quiet of the morning. Being happy is never simple in Algiers; even if all you have to do is clear out a bookstore and leave, it turns into an epic!

He gets back to work. In one of the books, *The Roundness of Days*, he finds a dedication: *To Edmond Charlot, in friendship, with thanks for taking care of* The Roundness of Days. *Jean Giono. August 1937.* He slips the volume into his suitcase. A present for Claire. Behind the shelves, he finds two black-and-white photos that have fallen down. One is of a group of men. On the back is an almost illegible inscription in black ink: *Amrouche, Fouchet, Roblès, Charlot.* The other shows a woman leaning against the trunk of a tree, wearing a broad-brimmed hat. On the back is written simply: *Manon Charlot.* He takes a bundle of a hundred or so subscription cards, their little blanks carefully filled out in a childlike hand—Abdallah's, he thinks—and dumps them in the trash.

Night is falling when somebody knocks. Outside, the neighbor's daughter, in her Mickey Mouse pajamas again, waves at him. When Ryad opens the door, she hands him a plate:

"It's from Mom. She said to bring you something to eat because you don't have anything and you'll starve to death and we should take pity on you."

"Well, tell your mother thank you from me."

"It's meatballs with tomato sauce."

Ryad devours the meal while eyeing the titles of the books at his feet. He rinses the plate in the little bathroom, climbs the stairs, and stretches out on the mattress fully clothed. He hears the roaring of a plane overhead. He imagines the big white shell and its passengers, the darkness in the cabin, the invisible trail in the night. Again he remembers Provence, with Claire and their group of friends. He remembers the sky full of stars, and Claire, hair in a mess, the end of her nose always red, her soft hands, bursts of laughter, rain suddenly falling on the beach out of nowhere, grilled fish, boiled fish, fried fish. In his thoughts, he walks over the sand, avoiding the big black rocks, to the start of a little path. There were flowers climbing up the wall of a house.

He can no longer hear the plane.

It's almost done. Ryad has dismantled the shelves. Only traces of dust are left to show that for years these walls were lined with books.

Abdallah is not out on the sidewalk. By the door, the horse-faced woman sprays her armpits with a fake perfume. Ryad watches her, disgusted. She notices and shouts:

"What are you doing? What do you want?"

Ryad says nothing.

"Pssscchhh! I'll blind you, you'll see, little pervert. Go on, that's it, get out. Say a word to anyone, and I'll tell my cousin in the army, and he'll get you sent to the desert, and you'll be eaten by a jackal, you little creep."

Ryad slips away through the alleys. For the first time since arriving, he feels that this corner of Algiers has some kind of charm. He passes empty stores, an elementary school that's closed, a municipal building on which a pasted sheet announces opening hours and reminds the people of Algiers that they must bring an identity card when making any kind of request. A gray car, a Renault, with two men in it, is keeping pace with him. Ryad glances at the men: mustaches, sunglasses, dark suits. He turns right; the car does the same. Annoyed, he steps into a big general store. He is jostled by a mother with a stroller full of children and packages.

He calls out to an attendant and asks for blue paint.

"What kind of blue?"

"Baby blue."

"I don't have any."

"Navy blue then."

"None of that either."

"Sky blue?"

"No, sorry."

"Periwinkle blue?"

"No, we don't stock that."

"Do you have some paint? Any color?"

"No. You know, kid, there's been a problem with the supply and delivery of paint for a while now."

"What about that big drum behind you with PAINT written on it?"

"Oh that? That's nothing. Just for display."

"OK, OK, forget it. Those blue boxes on castors, behind you, are they for sale?"

"Oh them, yes, you can have them."

Ryad heads back to the bookstore grumbling to himself. The horse-faced woman is gone, but the gray car, the Renault from before, is now parked in her place. The two men sitting in it are reading newspapers, with the motor switched off. Ryad fills the bucket, pours in some bleach, finds a rag, and covers the floor with newsprint and papers, which crunch underfoot. He starts washing down the walls of the store. Soon they're looking cleaner. The car remains on the pavement, oblivious to possible fines. When the sun goes down, Ryad decides, finally, to call it a day. He's hot from all the scrubbing and covered in sweat but he knows that outside the temperature has fallen. The musty odor has been replaced by a stink of bleach. He looks around and makes a mental list of what remains to be done:

Get rid of the books.

Throw out the shelving.

Throw out the mattress.

Throw out the desk and the chair.

Throw out the fridge.

Grab his things and go back to Paris to be with Claire, hoping all the way that she hasn't stopped painting her nails blue.

Kiss her.

Make her laugh.

He switches on the lights. A long time ago, in this place, he thinks, writers, poets, and painters stood. *Enough. All these stories are giving me a headache.*

He piles the books haphazardly into the blue boxes on castors. He pushes the boxes out the door and puts a sheet of paper on top that says: FREE, HELP YOURSELF, TAKE THE LOT!!!

The two guys in the gray car are watching. One of them, a cigarette hanging from his mouth, takes out his phone and makes a call. Ryad sets off for Chez Saïd. The black sky is like an enormous ceiling overhead, and the café seems farther away than before. He is weary, worn out, feverish. *I have to get this done.*

Abdallah is drinking coffee and reading the newspaper. Ryad sits down opposite him without a word. The evening clientele is more anonymous, noisier. Suddenly, a juddering rises from the depths of the earth: outside, a workman is breaking up the pavement with a jackhammer, while two others stare into the hole. After a few minutes, he takes a break. The men put down their tools, come into the café and make themselves comfortable. In the street: bearded men, groups of youths, children, animals, a little man lugging a huge flatscreen TV, an anonymous crowd of people going home. Some teenagers run by waving big Algerian flags, their faces painted green, white, and red. With a smile, Ryad watches them pass. They yell, dance, and sing. Cars honk their horns. The streetlamps flicker on, emitting a greenish light. Some no longer work; the bulbs are gone. Finally, Ryad breaks the silence:

"Interesting news?"

"Accident in a factory. A bad one. Three dead."

"What happened?"

"They don't know yet."

"Is there going to be an investigation?"

"There will be, for sure. You know, when I was eight or nine, there was a terrible accident on one of the colonial farms. An Algerian, a native as they said back then, was crushed by a faulty cart. Nourredine, he was called; he had three children. The cart tipped over, and he fell; it was awful. One of the wheels went over his body. At the time, we didn't have the right to an investigation. They said: That's just how it is; no one's to blame. And we buried the poor man."

"And you still remember it?"

"It was my first funeral! I'm ashamed to admit it, but at the time I found it all very exciting. The men seemed enormous, like giants. They knew exactly what to do: the body was wrapped in a white sheet; they lifted it up without trembling. Everyone looked sad, but I couldn't stop thinking about giants. I loved stories about giants. My mother was always making up tales to tell me. She told me that in the beginning the earth was inhabited by giants, but God shrank them down because they were bad. I knew I was supposed to be sad and pray for Nourredine, but I couldn't. There had been the wake with all the wailing and the tears, and the babies crying, and the women telling stories about the dead man and laughing. Those sounds had lulled me to sleep. The men were gathered outside, full of anger. They were smoking bad tobacco, stamping and jumping to keep themselves warm (that winter was bitterly cold), and wiping away the odd tear. My father let me go with him to the cemetery, in spite of my mother's protests: she thought I was too young, but I wanted to be with the men, and I felt so good, holding my father's hand."

"And why do you carry a sheet on your shoulders?"

"It's my shroud."

"Your what?"

"My shroud. The sheet I'll be buried in."

"That's horrible. Why do you lug it around with you all the time like that?"

"So I won't be a nuisance to anyone. The day God calls me, they'll be able to bury me straightaway, and I won't be a bother to my friends."

"But ..."

"When you get to my age and you're on your own, you'll understand."

The waiter refills their coffee cups and asks:

"Are you staying to see the match?"

"What match?" asks Ryad

"What do you mean, what match? The match today."

"Who's it against?"

"France. A friendly match, sparks are going to fly ... In five minutes' time the whole of Algeria will be in front of the television, cheering on the team."

"But we'll lose, won't we?"

"Shut up, you'll bring us bad luck."

The workmen look daggers at Ryad. The waiter announces:

"It's about to start!"

He turns off the lights. Kids bang on the table, yelling excitedly. Students order beers and gulp them down. Abdallah gets up, Ryad follows him. They move to the bar, "the best place to watch a match." The regulars, a handful of taciturn, sinister-looking drunks, have their eyes fixed on the screen. When the French team comes onto the field, there are boos from certain customers. To which others reply: "Hey shut up! Show some respect, you idiots." An old man, pretty far gone, it seems, harangues the kids who have painted their faces red, white, and green:

"You look like clowns."

"Listen, grandpa, don't you start up again."

"You're watching the soccer like faggots ... pfff."

"Shut up, will you?"

"I had some dignity, at least, in my time. And how can you go around with a haircut like that?"

"Enough, grandpa!"

"A great player, he was, one of the greats. But you don't want to learn anything, do you, bunch of idiots! The fourteenth of April 1958, I was what, fourteen. It was a month before the World Cup."

"Who cares?"

"Two men come into the hospital room where Rachid Mekhloufi is laid up: Mekhloufi, star striker for Saint-Étienne, the reigning champions. He's twenty-one ... How old are you? He was injured in the match against Beziers, the day before, so he's taking it easy. The two men are Mokhtar Arribi, coach of Avignon, you know Avignon? What? You kids know nothing! The other man is Abdelhamid Kermali, who plays for Olympique Lyonnais. All three are from Sétif. Since the massacres in May '45, things have been going round and round in their heads. They ask Rachid to join them in founding the Algerian national soccer team. He would have to leave France in secret, and give up everything: his friends, his hopes of playing in the World Cup. All to join a team that doesn't exist in a country that doesn't really exist either. Rachid says yes straight-away. The other two are thrilled. They've been told to give him money if necessary but Rachid asks for nothing. He's in the French army but he's prepared to desert and give up the idea of winning the World Cup. He's only twenty-one, did I say that? OK, all right."

"Are you going to shut up now?"

"There are ten of them altogether who make the same decision: they cross the Swiss or Italian border and make their way to Tunisia. The risk they took was huge."

"Shit! French goal."

"It was in all the papers: 'Nine French Muslim players from Algeria desert their teams,' 'The FLN team,' 'Algeria's fighting team.' Things went crazy. The secret hadn't leaked; nobody knew. Not even the FLN, apparently! It was in the news for three days, on radio stations all around the world. The French were furious. The whole world was hearing about us. When did that ever happen? The team that was formed on a sandlot went on to tour the world. Sixty-five victories. France pressured the FIFA to stop them playing, but plenty of countries ignored the ban. People loved the story, and it was moving to see those guys. They advanced the Algerian cause by ten years. That's not just what I think; I'm quoting Ferhat Abbas. You know who Ferhat Abbas is, right? The pharmacist from Sétif? I don't know what they teach you at school."

"Listen, grandpa, we don't give a shit about that stuff. Drink your beer and watch the match."

"You know, those kids gave up everything for an idea that could have failed. Some of them could have ended up in front of a firing squad. People in France at the time were calling them traitors. But they should have stopped to think, and asked themselves why young men with such bright futures would give it all away for a cause that France couldn't see the justice of."

Two half-drunk young men approach Abdallah and start touching his shroud.

"Oh, it's so soft, can I stroke it ... ?"

Abdallah pushes them away. A waitress steps forward to escort the louts from the premises. Her eyes are full of anger. She comes back to tidy and smooth the sheet, then kisses Abdallah on the forehead. He thanks her with a smile. She turns to Ryad:

"Hi, remember me? I'm Sarah. We met the other night, at Saïd's place, with my friends."

"Oh yes, and the blind man ..."

"Youcef."

"Youcef?"

"Youcef, not *the blind man*, jerk; call him by his name."

"Yes, of course. You know, that reminds me, I've got a whole lot of books to give away. Do you want to come and take some?"

"I'll come tomorrow and choose one or two: a bit of fun for Youcef."

She sits down beside Ryad to follow the match, her thigh against his. He can smell her warmth, the scent of her hair and skin. He tries not to look at her long auburn hair. She is wearing close-fitting black trousers and a shirt that is tight across her breasts.

* * *

It's halftime. Horns are honking, cars have filled the streets. Every now and then a human voice can be heard from one of the higher balconies. Ryad takes the opportunity to slip away. The gray car, he sees, is still there with the two men in it. Someone has taken the blue boxes but dumped their contents. The books are lying in the puddles, ruined for good. The smart aleck has even written THANK YOU on Ryad's notice and taped it to the window of Les Vraies Richesses.

Paris, 1961

The rain falls. The sky is gray. By the Seine, the wind blows hard. Children's hats, well-dressed girls, leather handbags, clean but mended clothes. Family groups and groups of friends. Some laughing, others serious. Together, we march to protest against the curfew arbitrarily imposed on Algerians in France.

Those Arabs. Those towelheads. Those rats. Those kebabs. Those turds. Those lice. Beat them. Slaughter them. Rub them out. Send them flying. Use batons. Use our police weapons. Use bricks. Kill as many as possible. Kill them by the dozen. Slaughter these people who have no right to be here in Paris, by the Seine, among our monuments, our trees, our women. Slaughter them. Beat them. Throw them in the river. See the Algerian bodies sinking into the muddy water. Far away now, the brown bodies. Make them disappear. Quickly. Brutal charges. Arab-hunting in Paris. Paris! Manned by Papon's police, Paris kills. Savage. Chases in the streets of Paris. Don't think twice: throw them over, into the Seine. Broken bodies. Beaten with rifle butts and batons. Bodies hung in the Bois de Vincennes. Seine full of corpses. Hate set free. Noise. Chaos. Baton blows raining on bodies lying flat, on bloodied skulls, on the unarmed. And the silence of the Parisians. Another charge. People on the ground. Blood everywhere. Ambulance sirens. More blows, and bodies in the Seine. A pogrom in 1961. Purify France of its Arabs. Disinfect the avenues. Slaughter the assassins. Repression. Tragic. Starting in the morning, Paris kills. The police, the riot squad, and the gendarmes are reinforced by the Auxiliary Police Force: brigades made up of Harkis, who fought with the French in Algeria. Zero tolerance. The arrests began even before the demonstration. Insults, blows, harassment. Made to swallow whole cigarettes. Water mixed with bleach. Brutal roundups. Blood on the Arab face. Broken legs. We hit, we unleash the dogs. We line the brownskins up against the walls. We pack them into police vans. We grab them in the street by their curly hair. We hunt the type. We throw stones. We drown them. For a whole month after, bodies will be pulled from the water. The killing will go on for days. Corpses in the Seine. Hands tied behind their backs. Strangled with their own belts. Bodies bound and flung into the water. When the families in Algeria are informed, they will not understand what has happened. Someone will bury the bodies somewhere. Paris!

Raided bars. Bludgeoning. Bullets in the head. Bodies piled into common graves. Bullets in the stomach. Bodies on the ground, hunched for protection. Iron bars and lead-tipped sticks. Paris! Systematic interrogation. Up against the wall. Faces drained of color. Pools of blood. Trembling hands. Wild eyes. The sound of the batons, the gun butts, the kicks. Arabs battered and hurled. Shot. Hundreds of men. In endless lines. Hands raised. Arrested. Beaten.

Night has fallen. Windows open. With heads full of rage and bodies spent, we let out heartrending ululations. A last salute to our dead.

On the 17th of October in the middle of the night, Claude Bourdet and Gilles Martinet, founders of *L'Observateur*, receive an unexpected visit from policemen who want to publish an anonymous tract. It will appear on the 31st of October: four pages signed by "a group of Republican police officers" who state: *What was done on the 17th of October 1961 and the following days to peaceful demonstrators, on whom no arms were found, obliges us to give our testimony and alert the public [...] All the Algerians caught in this huge trap were battered to death and thrown systematically into the Seine.*

Many years later, our grandparents will see us leaving the country to cross the sea, and they will tell us to be careful: "The French are hard." And we will not understand because we will have forgotten.

Edmond Charlot's Notebook
Algiers 1961

April 29, 1961

Unveiling of a stela in honor of Camus, designed by the brilliant Louis Bénisti and set among the ruins of Tipaza. They couldn't have put it anywhere else. Bénisti chose a sentence from *Nuptials* to be carved into the stone: *Here I understand what glory means: the right to love without measure.*

Deeply moved.

July 3, 1961

News of Amrouche. I'm told he's spreading malicious rumors about me, talking about embezzlement, telling Paulhan that I was "dishonest." When the gossipmongers start up, I try to make it clear that I'm not interested. Amrouche was a friend. Nothing else matters. *We were all friends and that's what it was, Éditions Charlot.*

September 5, 1961

Attack on my store in the Rue Michelet, attributed to the OAS. We think they were after someone else and got the wrong address. We're all right, but I lost about 20 percent of my stock.

September 7, 1961
I've started the repairs and the tidying up. Still in shock.

September 10, 1961
New door, fixed the shelving. Sent the family to France.

SEPTEMBER 15, 1961.
SECOND BOMBING
OF MY RIVAGES STORE.
THEY TOTALLY DESTROYED IT,
THE SWINE.

September 16, 1961

My store has been completely ruined. I've lost everything, absolutely everything: Camus's reader's reports, my correspondence with Gide, Amrouche, and the others. Thousands of books, documents, photographs, and manuscripts: all up in smoke. My precious archives gone! The second floor was blown away. All I have left are a few books and this journal. A whole life reduced to rubble. I'm reeling. What's the message? What was their target? Who were they after? The young man who published *Revolt in Asturias*, who wasn't even twenty at the time? The publisher of Vercors? Or of *Algeria Will Be French and Happy*? Was it the Resistance publisher, or the man who recently said in a café for all to hear that he was opposed to the bomb attacks that were killing Arabs every day? A friend to Momo and others? And Momo ... the bard of the Casbah, my faithful friend, who came to see me there, in the ruins, and slipped a roll of bills into my pocket: all his savings.

September 17, 1961

Storefront blown out, glass on the pavement. Grille ripped apart. Rubble and confetti.

I'll never have the strength to start all over again.

September 18, 1961

They've dug out about twenty tons of rubble and shredded paper. Camus's manuscripts, Giono's letters, the artwork for the magazines, all the books I've published since 1936, the books my grandfather left me ... rubble and confetti.

September 24, 1961

Not a cent left. Alone in Algiers with my rubble.

October 5, 1961

My family keeps writing from France: they want me to leave Algiers, but I can't. All this will pass.

October 12, 1961

Georges Drouet, director of the radio station France 5 Algiers, has come to my aid. He's employed me as manager of the news programs and artistic advisor.

October 19, 1961

A journalist who is preparing yet another article on Camus asked me if I had ever encouraged anyone to write. Plenty of people. I told him my method:

Buy a desk, the plainest one you can find, as long as it has a drawer that locks.

Lock the drawer and throw away the key.

Every day, write whatever you like, enough to cover three pages.

Slip the pages in through the gap at the top of the drawer. Without rereading them, obviously. At the end of the year, you'll have about 900 handwritten pages. Then the ball's in your court.

7

In the morning, Ryad counts the books left in the store: sixty. All the others are soaked. He puts the picture books aside.

That damned gray Renault is still there in the street. As he walks past, he thinks he sees a blue shape on the back seat. He threads his way through the alleys and finally reaches the elementary school where the little girl next door goes. He tells the guard that he would like to give the children some books. The guard scratches the top of his head, looks him up and down, and asks him to wait outside the gate. Ryad can see the yard through the grille. It's charming, with its vegetable bed and its soccer field traced out in chalk. Children are sitting on wooden benches sharing a secret, a piece of chocolate, or their dreams. A dark little boy in a striped T-shirt and overalls is trying to climb a pole. He keeps slipping down and landing on his bottom. But he tries again, undaunted.

Finally, the guard comes running back, accompanied by a man with a potbelly.

"Hello, hello. Yes, I hear you would like to donate some books."

"Yes, I'm clearing out a bookstore and I have some children's books."

"Ah, that's wonderful, really wonderful. I wish there were more people like you; your parents should be proud of you, you're wonderful."

"Thank you ... Really, it's nothing ... So I have about twenty books; I can bring them today."

"Look, I would really like to take them, but I'm afraid it won't be possible."

"Why not?"

"We're not allowed to accept personal gifts, you see?"

"Even books?"

"Yes, you never know."

"What don't you know?"

"So many things, oh, so many things! Who wrote the books, who published them, who printed them, who sold them, who brought them, who will read them ... No, no, it's really not possible."

"But I can't just throw them out. You can use them ..."

"Listen, write a letter to the inspector at the Ministry of Education. Wait for an answer; it might take a while, because it has to go to the committee. You have to be patient. Then you'll be able to bring the books."

"But ..."

"You go and do that. Good day to you, my son, and thank you again, the children will be glad to hear about what you tried to do for them."

The guard slams the door shut in Ryad's face. Now he is back in Rue Hamani. We see him walk past the damned gray Renault. He ignores the men who are spying on him night and day. He's not afraid of them and he's right: they won't do him any harm. They are only there to remind us that they exist and that we are all under surveillance.

Almost as soon as Ryad steps into the store, somebody knocks at the door. It's Sarah, radiant in denim overalls, with her auburn hair loose on her shoulders.

"Well, it's empty here."

"Yes."

"Do you know what they're going to do with it?"

"Yes, the owner is going to sell beignets."

"Beignets? Uhuh ... So I'm guessing these books on the floor are the ones you're giving away?"

"Yes."

"OK, I'll take the Jules Roy and this one by Mohammed Dib. Pass me the Houhou and maybe a Camus as well. I hope that's some help."

"You can't take anymore?"

"No, no, this is already too many. But listen, if you really want to get rid of them, take them to the underground lookout."

"The underground lookout?"

"It's in the old Rue Élisée-Reclus. Jean Sénac died there. You don't know who he was, do you? I can tell by your face. Sénac: a poet, a member of the FLN, a homosexual with a big beard. No, doesn't ring a bell? Kids get together there to write poetry and smoke and read. They'd be happy to have some books. I can take you, if you like."

Ryad fills his suitcase with books and follows the young woman. They walk along avenues, across squares, and finally end up in some kind of dirty alleyway. Sarah leads him toward a building with a skull tag on the wall:

"Go on, it's downstairs, I have to go, see you round."

Stepping into the entrance hall, Ryad pinches his nose shut. He doesn't dare switch on the light; he doesn't want to touch anything. He pushes the door open with his shoulder, heaves his suitcase, and enters the underground lookout. There are plates, bottles, glasses, notepads, books. The walls are covered with photos and drawings, illuminated by bare bulbs.

The place stinks of beer.

"Come in, come in. Make yourself at home."

The young man has a book in his hand. He is very fat, with a pudding-bowl haircut, and round, wire-framed spectacles.

"I'm a writer and a poet."

He looks up at Ryad with a blend of false humility and pride.

"Do you write? No, you don't, I can see that, what a pity," he sighs, before yelling out: "Ladies!"

Ryad starts. Three women turn toward him.

"Greet the gentleman who has come to visit us."

Intimidated, Ryad opens his suitcase without saying a word.

"Fantastic!"

They fall on the books, open them, stroke the covers, smell the paper. They have forgotten about Ryad, who takes this opportunity to slip away. As soon as he is in the street, torrential rain comes down. He runs to take shelter in Les Vraies Richesses. Because of the rain, he can't bring himself to throw out the shelving, because of the rain and Abdallah, who is still keeping watch, he knows, although today, again, he hasn't been there in the street. Ryad ends up going to bed without having dared to put the shelves and furniture out on the sidewalk.

The next morning, he opens the door and feels snowflakes melting on his open palm, flakes delicately falling on the silver, sparkling sea, on the wire fence of the elementary school, the tables outside Chez Saïd, and the trash bins in front of the underground lookout.

Ryad is tired of waiting. Winter will never end. It will swallow Algiers whole.

The shelves, the mattress, the desk, the chair, the fan, the rusty old sign, the photos, the fridge, the hot plate, and the big portrait of Charlot are all outside now. Standing on the opposite sidewalk with a look of desolation on his face and the white sheet wrapped around his shoulders, Abdallah watches his universe sinking. Ryad goes to join him.

"A few years ago. A woman came here. A little woman with blonde hair. She told me that Charlot had died, in Pézenas. It was a shock. In the old house where he spent his last days, he had gone almost blind, which made him terribly sad, because he could no longer read or write letters to his friends. He was cremated and his ashes were scattered over the Mediterranean, his 'home.' The lady also told me that he had been very happy to hear that this bookstore had been preserved."

The raindrops strike at the books with a sharp, military sound. People don't really live in places, Abdallah thinks, it's places that live in people. Ryad looks at the big sign, dripping with rain: "The young, by the young, for the young." He doesn't feel young anymore. His head is full of Abdallah's stories: those heavy stories that go to make up History with a capital *H*, but he doesn't know what to make of them. He feels that somehow he has failed to carry out his task. The portrait of Charlot is drowning in the waters of Algiers.

Watching Abdallah and Ryad through the foggy windshield of their gray Renault, the two men take notes.

Algiers, 2017

You'll go to Les Vraies Richesses, won't you? You'll walk up and down the steep alleyways. The sun will beat down; you'll stay in the shade. You'll avoid the hectic Rue Didouche Mourad—so many alleyways off to each side, like hundreds of intersecting stories—until you come out a few steps from a bridge that is favored by suicides and lovers alike.

You will stop at the terrace of a café and, without hesitating, take a seat and strike up conversations with the other customers. For us, here, there is no difference between the people we already know and the people we have just met. We will listen to you attentively and accompany you on your walks. You will not be alone anymore. You will climb the streets, push open heavy wooden doors, imagine the men and the women who tried to create or destroy this land. You will feel overwhelmed. And the blue overhead will make you dizzy. You will hurry, heart thumping, to Rue Charras, which now has a different name, and look for 2b. You will ignore the gray Renault parked on the pavement. The men in the car have no power. You will find yourself in front of the former bookstore Les Vraies Richesses; I imagined its closure but it's still there. You will try to open the glass door. The neighbor, who runs the adjoining restaurant, will tell you: "He's gone to lunch. He has to eat, too! But don't go, wait a bit, he'll be back. Here, have a lemonade."

You will sit on the doorstep, beside the plant, waiting for the attendant. He will hurry when he sees you. Finally, you will enter that little store, where so many stories began. You will look up to see the big portrait of Charlot, in his dark glasses, smiling. Not a broad smile, but it's like an invitation, as if he were saying: "Welcome, come in, take what you like." You will remember what Jules Roy wrote: "For me, what remains of that adventure, though we didn't perceive it as such at the time, is a sort of mirage. It was as if Charlot had created us all, or at least presided over our births. He was the one who invented us (perhaps even Camus); he brought us into the world, shaped us, coaxed us, told us off sometimes, always encouraged us, praised us beyond our merits, brought us together, smoothed us, polished us, set us right, fed us often, raised us, inspired us ... Never once did he say a word to suggest that our talent represented anything less than the future of Algerian and French and indeed of world literature. We were the finest poets, the brightest rising stars; we were marching toward a legendary future; we would bring glory on the land of our birth ... We were his dream. And then fate played a cruel trick on him, like a storm brewing over a calm sea. For as long as he could, he held out against the gale. I never heard him complain about his misfortunes or the injustice of his lot. Sometimes I wonder if we were really worthy of him."

One day, you'll come to 2b Rue Hamani, won't you?

SOURCES

A year of sifting through archives. Meeting Charlot's friends. Devouring books, interviews, documentaries. Most of all, revisiting the little yellow volumes published by Domens, which are like talismans, dipping into Charlot's memories, borrowing a few words here, a sentence there, embroidering, imagining. Finally, remembering the method that he recommended to aspiring writers. A generous method, like its inventor.

BOOKS

Fanny Colonna, *Instituteurs algériens (1883–1939)*, Les Presses de Sciences Po, 1975.

Jean Amrouche and Jules Roy, *D'une amitié. Correspondance Jean Amrouche-Jules Roy (1937–1962)*, Édisud, 1985.

Jules Roy, *Mémoires barbares*, Albin Michel, 1989.

Michel Puche, *Edmond Charlot éditeur*, Domens, 1995.

Jean-Claude Xuéreb et al., *Audisio, Camus, Roblès, frères du soleil, leurs combats. Autour d'Edmond Charlot*, Édisud, 2003.

Angie David, *Dominique Aury. La vie secrète de l'auteur d'Histoire d'O*, Éditions Léo Scheer, 2006.

Edmond Charlot and Frédéric Jacques Temple, *Souvenirs d'Edmond Charlot, entretiens avec Frédéric Jacques Temple*, Domens, 2007.

Hamid Nacer-Khodja, *Sénac chez Charlot*, Méditerranée vivante / essais, Domens, 2007.

Jean El Mouhoub Amrouche, *Journal (1928–1962)*, ed. Tassadit Yacine Titouh, Non Lieu, 2009.

Gaston Gallimard and Jean Paulhan, *Correspondance (1919–1968)*, ed. Laurence Brisset, Gallimard, 2011.

"Sortir du colonialisme," *Le 17 octobre 1961 par les textes de l'époque*, introduction by Gilles Manceron, afterword by Henri Pouillot, Les Petits Matins, 2011.

José Lenzini, *Mouloud Feraoun. Un écrivain engagé*, introduction by Louis Gardel, Actes Sud / Solin, 2013.

Bernard Mazo, *Jean Sénac, poète et martyr*, Seuil, 2013.

Guy Dugas, *Roblès chez Charlot*, Méditerranée vivante / essais, Domens, 2014.

François Bogliolo, Jean-Charles Domens, and Marie-Cécile Vène, *Edmond Charlot. Catalogue raisonné d'un éditeur méditerranéen*, Domens, 2015.

Michel Puche et al, *Rencontres avec Edmond Charlot*, Domens / El Kalima, 2016.

Guy Dugas et al., *Des écrivains chez Charlot*, Domens / El Kalima, 2016.

Guy Dugas et al., *Edmond Charlot, passeur de culture. Actes du colloque Montpellier-Pézenas. Centenaire Edmond Charlot 2015*, Domens, 2017.

ARTICLE
Sorj Chalandon, "Il y a du sang dans Paris," *Libération*, October 12 and 13, 1991.

FILMS

Frédéric Jacques Temple, Geoffroy Pieyre de Mandiargues, *Alger au temps des "Vraies Richesses,"* ADL Production, FR3, 1991, 52 minutes.

Michel Vuillermet, *Edmond Charlot, éditeur algérois*, Tara Films / ENTV, 2005, 52 minutes.

ARCHIVES

Letters of Jean Amrouche, Bibliothèque littéraire Jacques Doucet.

Dossier *L'Arche*, Robert Aron collection, Bibliothèque de documentation internationale contemporaine de Nanterre.

Dossier Éditions Charlot, Bibliothèque littéraire Jacques Doucet.

Gallica / BnF for newspaper articles from the period, and particularly the archives of *L'Écho d'Alger*.

Armand Guibert collection, "Patrimoine méditerranéen," Bibliothèque interuniversitaire de Montpellier.

THANKS

To Frédéric Jacques Temple, Guy Dugas, Jean-Charles Domens, Marie-Cécile Vène, and Michel Puche for sharing their stories with me.